Pippa Roscoe lives in Norfolk, near her family, and makes daily promises to herself that this is the day she'll leave the computer to take a long walk in the countryside. She can't remember a time when she wasn't dreaming about handsome heroes and innocent heroines. Totally her mother's fault, of course—she gave Pippa her first romance to read at the age of seven! She is inconceivably happy that she gets to share those daydreams with you. Follow her on Twitter @PippaRoscoe.

FROM ONE NIGHT TO DESERT QUEEN

PIPPA ROSCOE

MILLS & BOON

First published in Great Britain 2021
by Mills & Boon, an imprint of HarperCollins*Publishers* Ltd,
1 London Bridge Street, London, SE1 9GF

www.harpercollins.co.uk

HarperCollins*Publishers*
1st Floor, Watermarque Building,
Ringsend Road, Dublin 4, Ireland

Large Print edition 2021

From One Night to Desert Queen © 2021 Pippa Roscoe

ISBN: 978-0-263-28905-3

11/21

MIX
Paper from
responsible sources
FSC **FSC® C007454**

This book is produced from independently certified
FSC™ paper to ensure responsible forest management.
For more information visit www.harpercollins.co.uk/green.

Printed and bound in the UK using 100% Renewable
Electricity at CPI Group (UK) Ltd, Croydon, CR0 4YY

This was written during the break between Coronavirus lockdowns in the UK when, more than ever, I was reminded of the power of reading romance. The power to escape, the power to hope, to love, and to look to a brighter future with a happy ending.

So, this is for all the incredible romance authors, editors, copy-editors, cover artists, production staff, admin staff, publishers, retailers, bloggers, reviewers… All the individuals who help make romance available to us readers even in the hardest of times.

Thank you.

PROLOGUE

'I'M NOT SURE that I should go.'

'We don't really have much choice.'

'I don't want to leave you with Star and the rest of it…'

Star Soames's heart thudded painfully in her chest. She knew that her sisters would be absolutely mortified if they knew she was listening, but hated the way she had been lumped in with 'the rest of it'. As if she were a duty, a burden, just like the one the grandfather they'd never met—thankfully, as far as Star was concerned—had placed on them.

Star willed back the tears clouding her vision as she tried to concentrate on what Skye, the eldest, was saying.

'It should only be a couple of days. Fly to Costa Rica, get the map from Benoit Chalendar, come home. Simple as that.'

'Except he's not likely to have the map on him, Skye,' came the gently worded reply from

Summer, their youngest sister and the peace-keeper of the family.

'Okay, so add in a day to return via France and I'll be back before you know it.'

Star ran her thumb down the length of the thick gold chain of the necklace that they had found only yesterday, along with their great-great-great-grandmother's journals, in a hidden recess tucked behind a section of shelves that swung open at the flick of a notch in Catherine's library. Star preferred that name to the other names the smaller library had come to be known by, like *the women's library* or *the little library*, and she wasn't surprised that none of the male Soames heirs had ever thought to look there.

If anyone had ever suspected Catherine of spiriting away the family diamonds from her evil husband Anthony, it had never been more than a suspicion as generation after generation went half mad trying to solve the mystery of the missing jewels that must be worth a small fortune. It was as if every single subsequent Soames had let the sprawling Norfolk Estate run to ruin in order to chase a myth, including Elias Soames, the man who had rejected and disowned their mother before she'd even left her teens. Star shivered in memory of the image of his portrait hanging in the estate office, where she and her sisters had first heard the terms of his will. As the lawyer had read the fiendish requirements of the inheritance, Elias Soames had stared down at them like a Dickensian villain, for all that the painting could only have been made twenty years before.

Elias had given them only two months to track down the Soames diamonds. And if they failed? The estate would pass to the National Trust. Star nearly laughed. If it hadn't been for their mother, the girls might have given the estate to the Trust with their blessing, none of them wanting anything to do with such a twisted manipulation. But because of their mother...

'In the meantime, please keep an eye on Star. You know how she gets.'

How she gets? Star mouthed to herself, frowning, shifting away from the door, really not wanting to hear any more but unable to get far before hearing Skye carry on.

'I'm worried that she'll try and go after the next clue herself. Especially as it could be so…'

'Romantic?' both of her sisters chimed together, descending into fits of giggles. Star clenched her jaw. She'd read and loved romances for more than half her life, defended them more times than she could count and would continue to do so while she still had breath in her lungs.

'I just worry that she'd get herself into trouble. And we really can't afford to…we don't have the time to get this wrong.'

A stab of hurt cut through her. While she hated what her sisters were saying, they were right. She looked around at the library, through the window where the stars in the night sky blinked over the land that came with the estate. Land that, had Mariam Soames lived there, might have had the right postcode. A postcode that would have meant she'd have had access to the most successful treatment for her stage three cancer. But her small flat in Salisbury, near the New Forest, was about as far as possible from this sprawling estate with two wings and more than forty rooms and was very much in the wrong postcode. Star couldn't help but shake her head at the injustice of it, at the cruelty that meant life or death was based on income, savings or property location.

'We've already lost two weeks getting this far. But now we have the journals, now that you've decoded the secret message written in them, we have our first real start to finding the Soames diamonds. Benoit Chalendar has the map of the secret passageways in the estate, I'm sure of it.'

'Skye, even if you do get the map, then we still need to find out where on the map they are hidden and how to access it when we do find it. They're not going to be just lying in a corner of the secret passageways. And if we find whatever the next clue is while you're still away, then Star will *have* to go. I need to be here to meet with the potential buyer and you know that the clause insists that one of us stay in residence for the two months we have to track down the missing jewels,' Summer reminded Skye.

'Can you believe this is our life right now? On a treasure hunt for diamonds that have been missing for over one hundred and fifty years?'

'No more than I can believe that all this could

be for nothing if we don't find the jewels and the entire estate is handed over to the National Trust. And then we wouldn't be able to help Mum.'

Selling the estate was the *only* way that the sisters would be able to pay for their mother's medical treatment.

'You haven't said how you know this mysterious billionaire…'

Star listened for an answer, but none came from Summer.

'You know you can talk to us if you need to.'

'I know.'

Star listened as the footsteps retreated down the corridor away from the library before sinking into the ancient leather chair. Again, her fingers ran up and down the thick bronze twists of the necklace, the action comforting as the heavy rectangular pendant swung like a pendulum back and forth from where it hung. It hurt that her sisters didn't think she could do her part without getting into trouble. That they doubted her. But, instead of wallowing in self-pity, she saw herself like an Arthurian knight, brandishing her sword, battle cry at the ready, determined to fulfil her quest. Gripping the pendant in her fist, she swore that she would follow the next clue wherever it led and she *would* return proving her sisters wrong, she *would* help to save her mother.

CHAPTER ONE

KHALIF INHALED DEEPLY through his nose and out through his mouth. Repeating the action did nothing to dislodge the tension pounding angrily in his temples. He rubbed at his eyes, squinting against his thumb and forefinger.

Five hours.

Five wasted hours he'd sat in that room, while fifteen people stared back at him as coffee grew cold, sweets grew stale and the room had become so stuffy they'd needed to open a window.

Stalking down the corridor, he told himself that he just needed air. Fresh air. He wasn't running. He just needed a minute to himself. Which was why he was taking the staff routes through the palace, not the main ones. He was *not* hiding from Amin, his brother's—no, his *own*—assistant. He was simply ensuring the longevity of the bespectacled man's life.

Through the window, across the courtyard,

Khalif could see the tourists leaving the exhibition housed in the public areas of Duratra's palace. The sound of two boys laughing as they were chased affectionately by their mother cut through Khalif like a knife, transporting him back to a time when he and his brother had run rings around the palace guards.

Grief was like a punch to the gut. Swift, harsh, hot and angry. An emotion he could not allow to be seen now that he was first in line to the throne. Three years on from the terrible accident and he still caught himself noting something to tell his brother, wondering what Faizan would think, would advise. But Khalif wasn't sure what was worse, to do that, or for that to stop.

It was a visceral sense of wrongness. As if that day the world had shifted a few degrees. Grief felt like trying to push the entire world back into place, millimetre by millimetre. And nothing worked. Not even pretending that he didn't feel like an imposter. A substitute for his brother's throne, as if Faizan would just appear from around the corner, laughing at him, telling him it was all a joke and taking back the responsibility that he, unlike Khalif, had been taught to manage. But Khalif knew better than to believe in fairy tales and daydreams.

The urge to find the nearest bar and wash away the acrid taste of resentment and grief with a drink was strong. But he'd not touched alcohol or a woman since he'd received the news about his brother. He might have once been the spare, the Playboy Prince loved internationally and equally by women and newspapers alike, but he was now next in line to the throne. And each and every day had been a battle to prove his worth as he forged himself into a ruler that honoured his brother, his father and his country.

He skirted the corridor that ran parallel to the rooms that housed the large public exhibition on Duratrian history and rounded the corner to where the security suite for the public areas was located and came to a halt. All five security staff, two in uniform and three in plain clothes, were huddled round the monitor as if their lives depended on it. Adrenaline crashed through him, his body preparing for fight.

'What's going on?' he demanded as he entered the room, searching the bank of monitors lining the back wall for any sign of threat or danger to the royal family.

The way the men all started and looked as guilty as schoolboys would have been funny if his heart hadn't still been pounding in his chest, his pulse throbbing painfully in his neck as the adrenaline receded.

'Nothing.'

'Sorry, Your Royal Highness, Sheikh—'

'I know my name, Jamal,' Khalif ground out. 'What is it?'

A few more denials hit the air, too many shaking heads and hands, and even if that hadn't piqued his curiosity a flash of red caught his eye on the central monitor. The one that the men had all been staring at.

'What is…'

A tourist stood in front of one of the large paintings in the Alsayf Hall. Khalif cocked his head to one side as if that would make the image easier to see. The female figure was respectfully dressed, despite the relaxed attitude towards attire in Duratra, with a sage green headscarf that…

Again, there was the flash of red. The scarf had fallen back a little and a long, thick curl of fiery red slipped forward before the woman quickly tucked it back behind the folds of her hair covering. All this was done with an economy of movement and without taking her eyes from the painting. Without the distraction of the bright red hair, Khalif took in the rest of the woman.

The denim jacket she was wearing covered her arms and was folded back at the cuff to reveal a series of gold and bronze bangles that hung around a delicate wrist. The jacket was cropped at the waist so that the white and green striped dress that dropped all the way to the floor should have been perfectly modest had it not hinted at the mouth-watering curves of her—

He forced his eyes from the screen and looked to the men in charge of his family's security.

'Jamal, you're a married man,' he scolded as if he hadn't just been staring at the very same thing. 'I expected more from you.'

'It's not that—' the guard tried to justify.

'No, of course not,' Khalif interrupted with a half laugh, 'because your wife would have your balls if—'

'No, Your Highness, it's really not that… She's been there for an hour.'

'And?' Khalif demanded.

'No, she's been *there*, in front of *that painting*, for an hour,' Jamal clarified.

'Oh.'

Khalif returned his attention to the monitor, where the tourist still stood in front of the painting of Hātem Al Azhar, his great-great-great-grandfather. He frowned, wondering what it was about the painting that had enthralled her for *an hour*. Given that, on average, it took one harassed school teacher to ferry a group of unfocused seven-year-olds a total of fifty-four minutes through the first section of the exhibition on the history of Duratra—a fact he knew only too well since his father had deemed it necessary for him to spend his teenage summers working at the exhibition in an attempt to instil in him a respect for their country's history and an awareness of the importance of tourism. Instead, all it had done was broaden his pick-up lines to include several more international languages. That aside, it *did* seem strange that this tourist had spent so much time in front of one painting.

He felt a prickle of awareness across his skin as he realised that the men had regrouped around the same monitor as if drawn by a siren call. He turned to stare at them until they moved out of his personal space, some clearing throats and others grabbing pens to make useless notes on unnecessary bits of paper.

Khalif gave her one last look, trying to ignore the twinge of disappointment as he took his leave. At one time she would have been just his type.

Star looked up at the large painting of the man who had ruled Duratra over one hundred and fifty years ago and smiled. The patrician nose was broad and noble, the jaw line masterful. Even allowing for artistic integrity, Star was thrilled to see the handsome image of the man Catherine Soames had met after her doomed love affair with Benoit Chalendar.

She felt as if she could get lost staring into the deep penetrating eyes of her great-great-great-grandmother's second love, until the security guard she'd met when she first entered the exhibition that morning cleared his throat.

She turned and saw him gesture slightly to the clock on the wall.

'Wahed, I'm so sorry. I had no idea that so much time had passed!' She was shocked and annoyed with herself for being such an imposition. The exhibition should have closed fifteen minutes ago and Wahed had been so helpful showing her around earlier. She smiled her brightest and most sincere smile, leaving the room just before she could catch the blush that rose to his cheeks, and drifted towards the exit.

Her first day hadn't been a failure *exactly*, she thought as she made her way towards the exit. *Yes*, they were short on time, Star admitted to herself, but the ache in her heart from a sadly now familiar panic would help absolutely no one, certainly not her mother.

The day after Skye had flown to Costa Rica, Summer had decoded the second part of the hidden messages Catherine had left in her private journals to reveal a description of a special key that could be found in Duratra. The key would unlock the room where Catherine had hidden the Soames diamonds.

With Skye tracking down the map of the hidden passageways, Star felt with every ounce of her being that finding the key was the final step in finding the jewels. When they did that they would have met the terms of their grandfather's will and they could finally sell the estate and be able to pay for the treatment that would save their mother's life.

On the plane to Duratra, Star had read and reread the stories of Catherine's adventures in the Middle East while travelling with her uncle and his wife. Catherine's father had been convinced that being a companion to her aunt by marriage would keep her out of harm's way until she was ready to marry someone suitable.

Even now, Star smiled at the thought of what Catherine had managed to get up to under the lazy eye of her aunt, of the poignant relationship that had developed between Catherine and Hātem. A smile that slowly fell as she remembered reading of the heartache of the two lovers as they had been forced apart by duty.

But, despite that, after she had returned to England, when Catherine had reached out to Hātem to ask him to make a key of special design, he had created something marvellous: a key that could be separated into two sections that mirrored each other. When joined, they would open a special lock, but when separate they could each be worn on a necklace. He had sent Catherine one half of the key and the lock, and he—as Catherine had requested— had kept the other. To Star, the fact that Hātem would always have a piece of Catherine with him was, as her sisters mocked her constantly for saying, *so romantic.*

Her fingers went to the chain around her neck, patting the thick twist beneath the thin material of her dress, reassuring herself it was still there. Tomorrow, she would leave it in the safe of her hotel room. But for this first day she'd wanted it with her, as if perhaps somehow it would draw out its other half. She'd had no idea of its significance when she'd first picked up the necklace from amongst the journals in the hidden recess in the library. Only that she was drawn to it. And now she couldn't help but feel a little as if it had been fate.

As Star made her way down the brightly lit corridors of the exhibition halls, weaving around obstacles with unseeing eyes, even she had to concede that she might have become a little carried away by the romance of another star-crossed love affair involving her ancestor, but she would never regret coming to Duratra, no matter what.

She had already fallen half in love with the bustling, incredible, beautiful city. In the fifteen-minute walk between her hotel and the palace that morning she had been surrounded by impossibly tall apartment buildings and office complexes and passed sprawling open-air markets before reaching the ancient stone structure of the palace in Duratra's capital, Burami. It was a clash of modern and ancient, as sleek electric cars glided silently down tiny cobbled streets and animals carried food, silks and spices to stalls that also sold the latest mobile phones and music players.

Star marvelled at the feeling that she was walking in both the past and the present—that her steps filled the footprints left behind by Catherine herself. And whether that worked to add a layer of magic and mysticism to the mundane, Star wasn't sure that she minded because of how complete and whole that sense of interconnectivity made her feel. Not that she'd say so out loud, and certainly not to her sisters, who would laugh at her when they didn't think she could hear.

So, despite the fact that she hadn't managed to find any reference to Catherine's necklace, Star wasn't discouraged. Instead, she was looking forward to seeing Burami at night and was even more eager to return tomorrow for the next section of the exhibition.

She was so lost in her train of thought that she walked straight into something tall, broad, not very soft but most definitely clothed. And breathing.

'Oh, I'm so sorry. Really, so—' She started apologising before she looked up, which was probably a good thing because her words were cut short by just one glimpse of the impossibly handsome man staring down at her as if he was more surprised than she was.

Star immediately pulled her eyes from his as if somehow that could stop the searing heat flashing over her skin. She blinked a few times, hoping that would clear whatever had come over her. If she'd been asked in that moment what he looked like, she'd not have been able to answer for all the world. But something instinctual told her that she would have known if he'd been within one hundred feet of her. Even now she felt it, the waves of something more… physical than sight. More visceral.

Still unwilling to meet his gaze, and genuinely concerned about the power he seemed to have over her body, she tried to extract herself from the situation. 'I really am sorry. I genuinely didn't see you there, which does seem a little implausible given…' at this point her hand entered the fray and gestured to the rather large entirety of him '…all that. You see, I get a little lost in my thoughts sometimes,' she tried to explain, finally daring to lift her eyes. 'I'm Star and…' she resisted the need to look away and ignored the burning in her cheeks '… I'm clearly assuming that you speak English, which suddenly feels quite conceited.'

The almost minuscule twitch at the corner of his lips made her think that he might be smiling at her rambling and Star sighed in relief at the indication that he at least seemed to understand what she was saying. 'I hadn't meant to be this late, or get this lost. I was in the exhibition,' she said, looking behind her and frowning, unable to recognise the corridor she was in, 'and time just…' She bit her lip, shrugging, wondering why he hadn't interrupted her yet. Her sisters would have. The teachers she worked with would have smiled vaguely and just pressed on past her. But he was still there. She knew this because she was now staring fixedly at his chest, debating whether Dickens had been onto something with the whole spontaneous combustion thing.

But the longer he stood there, not saying anything, the more aware she became of...*him*. This was silly. Maybe she was overreacting.

'Star...'

Her name on his lips drew her eyes upward like a magnet and she was immediately struck by the sheer force of his gaze.

Nope.

She had *not* been overreacting. He was looking at her as if she had the answer to an unspoken question. She felt as if he were searching for something within her.

She shook her head, severing the strange connection, and slapped him gently on the arm. 'You *do* speak English,' she chided, peering over his shoulder for the exit and missing the look of absolute and complete shock that had entered the man's eyes, which he'd managed to mask by the time she returned her attention to him. 'You had me going there for a moment.'

'Sir—'

Star turned in time to see Wahed, his eyes bright and his cheeks red, rushing towards them, making Star think that she really had overstayed her welcome.

'Wahed, I'm sorry. I took a wrong turn and bumped into…' She turned back towards the man she had bumped into, deciding it was safer to look somewhere around the area of his left shoulder. And then became slightly distracted by the way his suit jacket fitted perfectly to the—

'Kal.'

She jerked her eyes to his briefly, before turning back to Wahed. 'Kal. Yes. Right. As I was saying, I got a bit turned around and couldn't find the exit, but I can see it now,' she said, spotting a green sign with white writing and an arrow that she could only presume to be a sign pointing to the exit.

Looping her arm through the arm of the man mountain she had crashed into, she determinedly dragged him with her as she made her way to the exit. She could *not* afford to get herself barred from the exhibition and, to avoid any more trouble, she was removing herself and this other tourist from the premises ASAP.

'Come on, Kal,' she said, passing Wahed, who looked a little as if he were about to explode.

Khalif was so busy processing the fact that this woman knew the first name of his security guard, whilst simultaneously calculating the number of royal codes of etiquette she had broken simply by touching him, that he did nothing to stop her from marching him halfway towards the fire exit that was for staff use only. But, even if he hadn't been, Khalif could not be one hundred per cent sure that he would have dislodged her tiny pale hand from his elbow. It was so small and delicate he feared he might break it.

He was still staring at it as they drew closer to Wahed, as if by studying the delicate fingers splayed across his forearm a second longer he'd be able to identify just why it was that something so small was sending enough electric currents across his skin to light the city of Burami for a month. And that was when he realised that it was the first physical contact he'd had with another person in nearly six weeks.

Obviously Khalif had not been under the naïve impression that he'd be able to continue his romantic liaisons while being first in line to the throne, but he'd not expected the strange social distancing effect the position would hold. Where once he'd have been able to slap Jamal on the back as he'd mocked him about his wife, now there was the painfully awkward renegotiation of power that still didn't quite sit right with him. And where once he'd have been more than able to remove the tiny pale hand from his elbow, now he seemed entirely incapable.

Wahed hadn't taken his eyes from Khalif, eyes that had grown rounder and wider the closer they came, sweat breaking out on the man's forehead as he clearly tried to figure out how to get his country's Prince out of the hands of this flame-haired pixie-sized bombshell.

'Goodnight, Wahed,' Star said as they drew level. 'I'll see you tomorrow,' she stated.

The look of panic increased on Wahed's features and Khalif had to look away in case he laughed and shamed the man even more.

'Tomorrow?' the guard asked weakly.

'Oh, yes, I've only covered the first part of the exhibition. I have three more parts to explore over the next three days,' she said, throwing the words over her shoulder.

'You're going to explore the exhibition for three more days…?'

Khalif couldn't be sure, but he was half convinced he'd heard an actual whimper from Wahed, who was now staring after them as Star continued to guide him towards the exit.

Unable to help it any more, Khalif allowed the tug on his lips to form a full grin and his chest filled with the need to laugh. It bubbled up, filling his lungs and pushing outwards, and he felt lighter than he had in weeks. Months even. Years… The thought was a pin pressed into a balloon as he realised it was how he had felt before. Before his brother had died.

'Did you like it?' she asked, having turned around, looking up at him and squinting in the late afternoon sun. She'd managed to get them out into the staff courtyard, where he saw Jamal peering at them through the window of the security suite.

'Like what?' he said, shaking his head to Jamal to signal that he didn't need their help.

'The exhibition,' she said, laughing again, as if she were half laughing at him and half with him. That sound, so light, so carefree, caught him like a physical blow. He was almost jealous of it. Her hand was still at the crook of his arm and he knew that he really needed to remove it, but he just couldn't bring himself to yet.

'Well, I don't want to give anything away. You still have quite a bit to cover.'

Rather than being disappointed by his answer, she seemed excited.

'Perfect! Please don't. I like surprises.'

Her face, upturned to the lazy yellow lowering sun, was a picture. Despite the expectation of green suggested by the red hair that was still just about tucked behind her headscarf, her eyes were blue—the dark blue of dusk.

'Star,' he said, understanding dawning on him.

'Yes?'

'No, sorry. I…'

I am never tongue-tied.

Pull. Yourself. Together.

'It's an unusual name,' he clarified.

She looked at him as if she could tell that wasn't what he'd intended to say. As if she could somehow sense things about him that he didn't want to share. That strange dusky blue of her irises seemed almost prescient. The dusting of freckles across her nose fanned out over her cheeks as if she'd been flecked with gold. He found himself leaning down towards her as if subconsciously trying to take a closer look, as if he was trying to count the freckles, as if there was something he was trying to work out about her but didn't know what.

'Yes. Even in England. And Kal?'

'It's…an old nickname.' It had only been used by his brother and Samira. He'd not said it or heard it for three years.

If she'd noticed that he hadn't answered her implied question and revealed the whole of his name she didn't seem offended by it. She turned to look beyond the railings surrounding the staff exit to the palace and frowned.

'I think perhaps this wasn't the exit,' she said as she finally let go of his arm and took a step towards the road that ran the length of the capital city.

'Do you know where you're going?' he asked. There was no way he could leave her in the middle of Burami—she seemed entirely capable of bringing about some kind of massive accident that would be sure to bring his country to a grinding halt for months.

She raised her hand to her eyes and looked out beyond the railings. He followed the direction of her gaze and clenched his jaw. In the distance he could see his father's sleek black motorcade making its way back to the palace and he felt the tightening of the steel bands of duty around his wrists.

'Yes. I can see the café there on the corner. That's the road my hotel is on. It's a...' She turned to look up at him. 'It's a nice café. If you'd...' She shrugged as if hedging her bets as to whether to finish the sentence or not.

He looked away, hiding just how much he wanted to say yes, from both her and himself. He smiled sadly and by the time his gaze had returned to those eyes understanding had dawned in them. 'Please take a car to your hotel. You are safe in Duratra. But perhaps Duratra is not safe from you,' he said. It was meant to be a tease, a light exchange before he left, but it had come out differently. It had been a warning from a man who was the embodiment of his country.

Dusk descended in her eyes and for a moment it was as if she had understood. And then the smile was back in place, the one that had hypnotised all the palace staff she had encountered—and he could see why.

She nodded and he watched her walk away, just as a gust of wind pressed the white-and-green-striped dress against the back of her legs, causing an explosion of erotic thoughts until Khalif's father's car turned the corner and grim reality intruded.

CHAPTER TWO

FOR WHAT FELT like the hundredth time that day, Star forced herself to reread the English translation of the description of how Duratra had been one of the largest academic centres during the height of the Ottoman Empire. But she just couldn't concentrate. Instead of finding clues or traces of Catherine or the necklace within the paintings and history of this beautiful country, she was hoping to see Kal—despite being aware of how unlikely it was.

She'd gone over and over their encounter in minute detail from the moment she'd left him in the courtyard until her latest breath. Although she'd initially thought him a tourist like her, she now thought that perhaps he worked at the palace. While she'd not wanted to give Wahed a reason to ban her from the palace exhibition, she now wondered if Wahed and Kal knew each other. Not that she'd asked the security guard when she'd seen him that morning.

No, sometimes it was better not to know, because this way she could imagine him as the undercover Prince of a neighbouring kingdom, here on a top-secret mission. Perhaps he was trying to correct some great wrong and he would need her help escaping Burami and together they could ride off into the desert and...

And then she laughed out loud at herself, not noticing how she had startled the other people in the very quiet room. She had never ridden a horse and couldn't imagine that riding bareback would be comfortable. But being in his arms? Once again, Star felt herself flush from head to toe. Looking at him had been like looking at the sun. Heat. All-consuming heat that she'd had absolutely no control over whatsoever.

No one had ever had that effect on her. She'd read about it so many times but had honestly thought it just a metaphor. She'd wondered at it, had brought out the memory of him standing there, searching her face, her eyes and *whoomph!* Head to toe. Every time. Even now she felt that pink heat stain her cheeks and, lost in her own world, fanned her face, nearly taking out a large German tourist with her elbow.

As she moved further into the room, golden glints and rich magentas caught her eye and she came to stand before a tapestry that took up nearly the entire length of the room. It was exquisite in detail, despite the clear effects of age, inscriptions flowing beneath the images, and instead of fighting for space at the explanatory plaque, Star wanted to stand back. Take it in, just as it was.

She wondered whether Catherine had ever seen this, whether she had stood looking at it, searching for meaning the way that Kal seemed to have searched her eyes. She forced her mind away from him and onto the fact that she was on the second day of her search.

Time was running out for Star to prove to her sisters that she could play her part, that she could travel to the other side of the world without needing their support, protection or concern. Why couldn't her sisters trust her when she regularly and successfully managed to take care of a class of thirty seven-year-olds?

She and Summer had decided that if there was no sign of the necklace she would return to Norfolk no matter what. From there, the sisters would decide together what to do next. If any more travel was needed, they would apply to Mr Beamish, the estate's lawyer, and he— as stipulated in the will—would fund whatever expenses were needed during the two-month period. Well, one month and just over one week now, Star thought, doing the maths.

Thirty-eight days. Her heart began to pound in her chest. It was the bass-line that beat beneath the layer of faith and hope she held in her heart. Constant, exhausting. She hated it and needed it. Because while that deep thrum in her heart was there, so was her mother, so was the chance that she'd be able to find the necklace. That she and her sisters would be able to find the diamonds, sell the estate and access the medical treatment Mariam Soames needed... and Star wouldn't lose her only living parent.

A flash went off, slicing through the rising panic in Star's chest, and Wahed crossed the room to speak to the German tourist's wife, who had clearly ignored the sign that said no photography. Before the argument could get heated, Star made her way back out of the room to one of the larger areas, looking for somewhere she could...breathe.

She was trying to find her way out when

the hairs on her arms lifted and heat broke out across the back of her neck. She paused, eyes closed, just feeling her way through that moment. Her pulse thudded in her ears for such a different reason than just seconds before, and when she opened her eyes and saw a figure marching down the corridor ahead of her, her heart raced. Instead of continuing down the hallway, he cut to the left and entered the beautiful green courtyard on the other side of the large glass wall that separated the corridor from the exhibition space.

Star placed a hand gently against the glass, the smooth cold surface sucking the heat from her skin. It was one thing to bump into a man and a whole other thing to approach him. She should go back to the public area of the exhibition. She should absolutely do that.

Khalif leaned back against the wooden bench, feeling the sun on his face, eyes closed, remembering the way that Star had done something similar yesterday. Why couldn't he get her out of his head? All the way through the council update with Reza, Duratra's Prime Minister.

'If I didn't know better,' he'd joked, 'I'd ask who she was.'

Khalif's grunted reply had been as non-committal as he got with his oldest friend.

All that morning he'd caught himself looking at his arm where her hand had been, remembering the way that her laugh had cut through him, recalling his last sight of her. It didn't help that he knew she was here. Somewhere in the exhibition. It was as if his body had been in a heightened state ever since he'd reached the lower level of the palace and he bit back a curse. He was worse than an untried schoolboy, lusting over his first crush.

Until the last hour, during a meeting with the Secretary of State for His Majesty Sheikh Abbad Al Jabbal. Samira's father had found fault with nearly every suggestion that the team had put to him. Not that Khalif could blame him. He knew they still hadn't come up with the best way to honour their loss. When it came down to it, there certainly wasn't a *right* way. There was nothing right about the deaths of his brother and sister-in-law, so why should their memorial be? Khalif braced himself against a shockwave of grief that sent out invisible ripples of incomprehension and pain, refusing to bend to it, to go under.

'Funny meeting you here.'

Khalif's eyes shot open and he stared at Star, standing in the centre of the courtyard as if she'd just magically appeared.

'How did you…?' His words trailed off as he saw the commotion gathering on the other side of the glass at the corner of the east wing. Several dark-suited guards were reaching for their weapons, ready to storm the courtyard. He threw a glare their way, wondering how on earth this English girl had slipped undetected past his usually highly efficient bodyguards. He held his hand out to stop them intruding and turned back to Star, who was still looking up at him, thankfully having missed the exchange.

'I hope that's okay… I just… I saw you and you looked…' She shrugged, not quite finishing her sentence.

She looked around the space, giving him time to take in the dark blue cotton headscarf, grey floor-length skirt and white top she was wearing beneath the same denim jacket, so very different to the glitz and glamour he'd seen throughout Europe's most fashionable destinations. But, instinctively, he knew that hers was the face he would remember in years to come. Her bangles clinked slightly as she moved forward to smell one of the plants in the giant urn in the centre of the courtyard.

As he listened to her inhale, he forced his eyes away from her and instead took in the scene he'd been blind to until she'd appeared. Four separate areas were full of thick green foliage and he would always associate this courtyard with the oasis his family used to visit in the desert.

'...hungry.'

'Excuse me?' he asked, dragging his eyes and awareness back to Star.

'You looked hungry,' she replied with a smile.

'Really?' he asked, surprised.

'Aren't you?'

'Well, yes, but...'

Star sat down beside him and began to unpack the large canvas bag she'd had slung over her shoulder. An impressive glass-bottomed lunch box landed between them on the bench. A flask of something was soon propped up against it, while she passed him a smaller box with the instruction, 'Can you open that?'

He found himself once again staring blankly at her before recovering and doing as she'd asked, the traces of yesterday's smile returning to his lips. It had been so long since someone treated him like an equal, he was determined not to break the spell.

He lifted the lid from the box she'd handed him and the smell of parsley and coriander and rich tomato sauce hit him hard, making his mouth water. He stared at the *mahshi* in wonder.

'Where on earth did you get this?'

'Oh, the chef at my hotel,' she replied, reaching over to take one of the courgettes stuffed with rice and vegetables. 'He promised that he didn't mind making it for me.'

'Of course he didn't,' Khalif replied, thinking that she could probably talk the birds down from the sky as easily as getting a chef to make her whatever she wanted. He bit into the courgette he'd helped himself to and groaned. Hats off to the chef. He really hadn't realised how hungry he was until she'd asked.

'We were talking last night and he was telling me about…'

He let her voice trail over him as he cast an

eye back to where the security detail had come up against Amin, who seemed almost apoplectic that he'd taken food from a stranger. Khalif didn't really know what he was so angry about. Amin would probably prefer it if there *was* poison in the food. That way he'd be able to fulfil his royal duties without the hindrance he clearly saw Khalif as being.

He cast an eye back to Star, still talking but looking ahead of her and gesturing expressively with her hands, clearly missing the way that the thick tomato sauce was dripping perilously close to his trousers. Khalif supposed that she could be a spy sent to poison him—if it hadn't been for the fact that there had been no threats to either the country or the royal family in over one hundred years. Faizan's helicopter crash had been investigated by both Duratra and an international investigative team and both had confirmed that a mechanical fault was to blame. Accidental death. Somehow the term seemed cruel, especially for the twin daughters he and Samira had left behind.

'And so, after a few failed attempts, it was decided I should probably leave it to the professionals. But it's so delicious I just couldn't refuse,' she said, handing him a piece of flat-bread and the little porcelain pot of hummus. She'd managed to convince the chef to make her a packed lunch with breakable china? He stared between the little pot and the redhead, who seemed utterly oblivious to the impact that she had on those around her. And suddenly he envied her that. No second-guessing and doubt-ing the impact of every single move, look, step, decision or indecision. As he scooped some of the hummus topped with beautiful pink pearls of pomegranate and flecks of paprika onto the flatbread, he saw his assistant throw his hands up in the air and as the taste exploded on his tongue Khalif decided that frustrating his par-ticularly sanctimonious assistant was a small victory in an otherwise complete failure of a day.

'That was the best *mahshi* I've ever had,' she sighed, leaning back against the wooden bench.

Khalif laughed. 'Had a lot of *mahshi*, have you?'

Star nodded, her smile lighting up eyes that were a touch lighter than they had been yester-day. 'Yup. My mum, she's…some would call her *alternative*,' she said in a half whisper, as if confessing some great sin. 'But she travelled a lot when she was younger and that influenced her cooking. We're all vegetarian so we do a lot of cooking ourselves. That, and we didn't have a great deal of money growing up,' she announced without the resentment that usually weighed down such a statement.

'What do they do? Your parents,' he clarified, unable to resist going in for one last mouthful of the hummus.

She should have known it was coming. Usually she could feel it building in a conversation, but with Kal it had taken her by surprise so she hadn't been ready for the swift pain that nicked her heart. 'My father died when I was a few months old, but he was a carpenter.' She rubbed her hands unconsciously, as she often did when she thought about her father, imagining the calluses on his hands that her mother had told her about.

'That must have been very hard. I am sorry for the loss you have felt.'

Rather than shy away, this time she wanted to feel the burn, the flame that was lit when Kal looked at her, even if she felt guilty for welcoming it to avoid that ache, but instead what she found in his eyes… Her heartbeat thumped once heavily in sympathy.

'And I am sorry for yours.'

He frowned, his head already beginning to shake, but she stopped him with her hand on his arm.

'I'm sorry if that was intrusive. I don't know who or…' she trailed off '…but I can tell.'

Kal nodded once. It was an acceptance of her offered comfort, but a definite end to the moment. Seizing the threads of the earlier conversation and definitely not ready for him to leave just yet, she pressed on. 'My mother has done lots over the years, but currently she's into candle magic.'

She folded her lips between her teeth, waiting for the inevitable reaction.

'Wait…candle what?'

'Magic. It keeps her happy and there is harm to none, so…'

'Alternative, huh?' he said, wiping his hands on the napkin she'd found tucked beneath the boxes, and she would have replied had she not been distracted by the way he smoothed the cloth across his skin.

'You're the youngest?'

She turned to him, curious as to how he knew that she had siblings.

'You said "we're all" and you don't strike me as an only child,' he explained.

'I'm the middle. Skye is older, and Summer is younger.'

'And do they all have…?' He waved his hand towards a strand of her hair that had come loose from her headscarf.

Laughing, she tucked it back safely behind the stretchy jersey. 'No, just me. Skye's hair is a dark brown and Summer's is cornfield blonde.' She could see his mind working, trying to do the maths, and took pity on him. 'Technically they're my half-sisters. But I'd never call them that.'

'Different fathers?'

She could tell that he was trying to keep his tone neutral and she appreciated it. Not everyone was that considerate. 'It certainly drew a lot of unwanted attention and judgement when we were younger, and a *lot* of stares.' Her sisters thought she hadn't noticed, but she had. Long before her grandparents had made their feelings known, Star had been aware of the way neighbours and some of the school parents and, in turn, their children had treated them, judged them, excluded them.

'Ahh.'

She cocked her head to look at him, as if the different angle would reveal more than he'd done already. 'You know how that feels?'

'A little,' he admitted. 'Different reason though.'

Star looked him up and down, noticing the sharp cut to his clothes, the thick, heavy gold watch at his wrist, the expensive sunglasses sticking out of his pocket and smiled kindly. 'Rich parents?'

'Something like that.'

'Rich *and* powerful. I *am* impressed,' she assumed. He barked out a laugh and she felt as if she'd won something precious. 'Children can be unintentionally cruel,' she said, thinking of the young charges she loved working with.

She sighed heavily, feeling very far away from her teaching assistant's job in the New Forest, and allowed herself a moment to bask in the sun. The warmth of it on her face, the feeling of contentment was tinged with a little something more. She hadn't realised how much of a relief it was to talk to someone. Okay, so she might have been talking *at* him, but still. Without opening her eyes, she drew his image to her mind, surprised how easily it came after the difficulties of yesterday. She mentally reached out to trace the strong jaw line shadowed with a close-cropped beard, imagining the feeling of him releasing the tension that she had seen when talking about loss. Unable to help the way her thumb stretched out to press against the plush lower lip, fire burning her thumb and core. The skin on her cheeks began to tingle, as if she had been stroked, and she leaned her head into the invisible touch, opening her eyes to find Kal staring at her, sending a jolt of pure lightning to her heart.

But, rather than turn away, embarrassed at being caught staring, he seemed to focus only more intently now that her eyes were open. A moment that she would hold to her as more precious than any romance book and she wondered for just a second if he might kiss her. Then he blinked and the haze of desire was banked.

'Where have you reached in the exhibition?'

She took a breath and grounded herself, taking a second to focus enough to remember where she had been. 'The attempted occupation by the Ottomans.'

'Ah. A Particularly violent and difficult period.'

'I should think so too. His Majesty Sheikh Omar could hardly allow the kidnap of his daughter to go unpunished.'

No, he could not, Khalif echoed silently, wondering what Star would think if she knew that, rather than being kidnapped, the family rumour was that Omar's daughter had run off of her own volition to be with a Turkish prince and unwittingly nearly started a war.

'And tomorrow?' He cursed the question that had fallen from his lips before he'd had time to think it through. He really shouldn't care what she had planned for tomorrow.

Star smiled excitedly and it rivalled the sun. 'Tomorrow is the Fatimid period.'

'History interests you?' he asked, unable to curb his curiosity.

'Yes, I like to see how everything comes together. How one generation impacts another,' she said, the blue in her irises deepening.

'What are you looking for?'

'Who said I was looking for something?' she asked a little too quickly and his eyes narrowed at the shift in her tone. He waited her out and, as expected, she clarified. The English were very predictable. 'Research.'

'For?'

'A family thing.'

And then, before he could stop her, she'd leaned over, clasped his wrist, turned it in her hand and read the time on his watch. It was not sensual, no trace of practised flirtation, it was perfunctory and over in a matter of seconds, but those seconds had branded him like molten metal.

'I have to get back. I need to find out what happened to His Majesty Sheikh Omar's daughter before it closes for the day,' and, before he could say goodbye, she'd slipped through the doorway, passed the seven large suited men, none of whom could take their eyes off her, and disappeared into the exhibition.

That night, Star returned to the hotel after discovering that Omar's daughter had been forced to marry a Turkish prince and felt the sting of injustice of a marriage not born from love. She sighed, thinking of Catherine's marriage to her horrible cousin, a man whose sole interest was property and diamonds.

He has always coveted them. The estate and the jewels are almost an obsession for him. And though society deems him worthy of my hand in marriage, I do not deem him worthy of them. They are the only part of the estate entailed to the female line and I will keep it that way.

She had read Summer's translations of the coded messages over and over again since they had first found them buried within the pages of her journals. For Catherine, Omar's daughter and even her own mother, marriage had been nothing more than a shackle. But…for her? Secretly, she'd always thought that she'd quite like to be married. To have a wedding and stand beside someone who told the world how much she was loved. To be claimed publicly, completely. And though she'd never admit it to her mother, Star couldn't help but wonder if her life might have been different had her parents married before he'd died, whether that might have changed the minds and attitudes of her grandparents, whether they could have been a positive part of her life rather than…

Star cut off that train of thought before it could take hold, turning instead to wonder if she should call Skye in Costa Rica. She was halfway through her time in Duratra and she was beginning to lose the confidence that she'd arrived with. She had only two days left and it was getting harder and harder to ignore the inner voice wanting to know what would happen if she didn't find the necklace, and what that could mean for her mother. But if she admitted as much to Skye, she would only tell her to go home and Star wasn't ready to hear that. She could call Summer in Norfolk, but she didn't want to hear her sister's gentle voice reassuring her that it was okay, that it had always been a long shot to send her to search for the necklace.

Star drew air into her lungs to cover the hurt and turned in the bed onto her side, closing her eyes to see Kal's staring back at her, eyes crinkled with the hint of that enigmatic smile and the light of…interest? Was that what she saw in his gaze? Was that what made her heart beat faster? What made her feel a little sick in her stomach at the thought of seeing him tomorrow, but feel even worse at the thought of not?

Two days, she reminded herself, she had two days. Though this time when she delved into what it was that made her heart beat like specks of sand dropping through an hour glass, it wasn't thoughts of Kal, but the fear of not finding the necklace.

After lunch in the courtyard, and after thoroughly reprimanding a slightly sceptical security detail, Khalif had surprised himself by managing to make some headway in the afternoon. He'd looked for her as he'd left the palace, but Wahed had informed him that Star had already left. Yet knowing that she'd be there the following day made him feel…as if he had something to look forward to.

So it had been a shock to discover that the depth of his reaction to *not* seeing her the next day was nothing short of painful. A sense of panic had risen within him. Panic that he'd never see her again, never find out what she was looking for, never see the accidental chaos that seemed to follow in her wake, never feel that sense of inexplicable peace he'd found in her company... He'd caught himself looking down corridors, purposely walking past the security suite to see if the guards were watching her again. Tempted, so very tempted to ask if they had seen her.

By the time he'd reached the afternoon of what he knew to be her last day at the exhibition, he'd convinced himself that such an extreme reaction indicated that it could only be a good thing that she was gone from his life. What did he think he could do if he saw her again anyway? Only that thought sent up a cascade of sensual imagery that he shut down before it could cut him off at the knees. He was no longer able to indulge in such whims. There was a plan. In three years, when he had proved himself the steady hand that would provide for his country until his nieces came of age, then a suitable bride would be found. And that suitable bride would *not* have flame-coloured hair and eyes so dark blue they were almost regal.

So as he left his office that evening he was halfway through congratulating himself for having survived a temptation called Star when he came to an abrupt halt. The gods were either laughing or punishing him.

Things might have been different if he had found her anywhere else in the palace. But Star had found the one spot that was sure to pack an emotional punch. The three steps looked deeply insignificant, and probably would have been to anyone else. But to Khalif they were painfully familiar.

He had spent just over seven hundred hours waiting for his father and brother on those steps. Despite having been largely excluded from the lessons Faizan had been required to have from their father on matters ranging from governance and international policy to languages and business studies, he'd thought he could wait them out. And his stubborn streak had lasted for two hours, every day for an entire year.

In that moment he knew what he should do—and what he shouldn't. His Highness Sheikh Khalif Al Azhar walked on, past the security suite, through the exit of the palace and towards his evening appointment with Duratra's council.

Kal, however, stood before a beautiful woman and heaved a sigh of relief.

'You know it all turned out okay in the end,' he said as he stood between her and the sun, her body enshrouded by his shadow. She looked up at him with huge ocean-blue eyes. 'That's the problem with looking at the history of a country backwards. Really you should have started with the Umayyad period, it's especially beautiful, given the metalwork and textiles.'

The smile that spread across her features chased the watery sparkle from her eyes. 'Perhaps you should have been my tour guide.'

'I would have been honoured,' he replied, surprised by the sincerity in his tone. 'You are leaving?'

'Tomorrow.'

'And you don't want to go?' he asked, wondering why that seemed to make her sad.

Her smile wavered. 'I want to see my sisters, and my mother, but… I didn't find what I was looking for.'

'Anything I can help with?'

He would have sworn on his crown that he felt the weight of her sigh. 'No, sadly not.' And he would have given it away to lighten that load.

'So, what are you going to do with your last few hours in Duratra?'

The shrug that barely moved her shoulders an inch was enough to drive him to action. He liked the tumble and roll of her words, the way they wound through his mind, treading down a path to wherever they wanted to go.

All Star could think of was the necklace. She had genuinely thought that she'd find it, and to not have found a trace or clue as to where it might be was devastating. She had let her sisters down. And, worse than that, her mother… She felt a wave of hurt crash over her anew, breaking out in a hot sweat on her neck and down her spine. She'd just got off the phone with Summer. And she'd meant to tell her, intended to explain that she would be coming home empty-handed, but Summer had been full of excitement with the news that Skye had found the map.

Star's phone was full of the pictures Summer had forwarded with promises that she would work on the plans to find where on the map the Soames diamonds were located. And at the end she had asked, hopeful for the first time since Star had got on the plane to Duratra, whether she might have located the necklace. A hope that Star had been unable to respond to. She had proved them right—that she couldn't be trusted to locate the necklace. How silly was she, to think that she could have done this alone?

All she wanted to do was stop for a moment. To not have to think, or fear, or worry. And although Kal had extended an offer of sorts, she'd sensed how torn he was. He probably had something to rush off to. And she certainly didn't want another person having to look out for her.

'Is there anything you haven't seen? That you wanted to?'

'Well, I've spent all my time here, so—'

'Wait, you've not seen anything of Burami?' he demanded, full of not *completely* mock outrage that distracted her heart just a little. Perhaps for the evening, rather than being a daughter hoping to save her mother, she could just be a tourist on her last evening in Duratra?

'Not unless it was between the hotel and the exhibition at the palace,' she replied.

'We can't have that.'

She couldn't help but laugh at his conviction. 'My flight is tomorrow—how much can you show me before then?'

'I can show you it all.'

He held out his hand and while she couldn't explain it, was helpless even to resist, Star felt as if she were Alice about to fall down the rabbit hole.

CHAPTER THREE

HAVING BEEN PROMISED the opportunity to see Burami, Star was surprised when, instead of turning out towards the main road, Kal led her back to the palace. The surprise lasted only a moment. She was distracted by the way sparks flew from where his palm pressed against hers, encompassing it, making her feel comforted in a way just seconds ago she'd not thought possible.

They came to a corner and Kal pulled up short before turning back to her, holding a finger to his lips.

Star folded her own lips between her teeth, but still a smile pulled at the edges of her mouth. 'Are we sneaking into the palace?' she whispered to him.

'Yes,' he replied, peering around the corner to see if the coast was clear.

'You do this often?' She couldn't keep the laugh from her voice this time.

He looked at her, eyes blazing with something a little more than humour. 'More than you'd think,' he replied cryptically and drew her back into the hallway.

They'd made it about four feet towards the staircase Kal seemed to be heading for when they heard the hushed voices of two guards. Eyes wide and heart pounding in her chest, Star didn't know whether to laugh or scream in fright. Either way she was pretty sure that she'd squeaked when Kal spun her round, pressing her back against a wall, arms braced either side of her head, and covered her with his body.

Star wasn't laughing now. They were staring at each other as if that alone would keep them invisible from the palace guards. This close, she could see that there were flecks of gold in the rich espresso depths of his eyes, she could almost taste the smoky sweetness of the breath that fanned gently against her skin. She dared herself to inhale the scent of him, woodsy, masculine, brought to her from the heat of his body. In her peripheral vision she could see the flicker of his pulse just beneath his jaw, and shockingly she wanted to place her palm there, to feel it beat in time with her own.

His head dipped ever so slightly towards her, his nostrils flaring ever so slightly, his inhale expanding to close the space between their chests from inches to millimetres. Beneath the voices, she could hear footsteps coming closer and closer. She pressed into the wall as if that would make her and Kal invisible, adrenaline reaching deeper and deeper into her bloodstream. What would happen if they got caught? Her eyes flew to his, her mouth opening just slightly as if ready to ask the question when she felt the pad of his thumb against her lower lip, just as she'd once imagined doing to him. The gesture she was sure was intended to stop her words, not her heart, but that was the effect.

She wanted to bite down on his thumb, to anchor it there before he could remove it and in an instant any fear was completely consumed by exhilaration. She'd never felt like it before. She could just hear the sound of footsteps over the pounding of her pulse in her ears, and she couldn't resist courting danger.

'Are we going to get into trouble?' she whispered against the pad of his thumb, instantly gratified when she saw his pupils flare.

'No,' he whispered back with an arrogance that was utterly devastating.

The footsteps receded, and Khalif waited until there was complete silence in the corridor. Not because he couldn't move, he sternly assured himself, but because he was waiting until the coast was clear.

He walked on into the hallway, leading Star by the hand, his heart racing, half hoping someone would stop him, half hoping they wouldn't. This was ridiculous. And certainly the first time he'd sneaked a woman *into* the palace rather than out of it.

Four feet to the staircase. He could still change his mind. Could still turn back.

Three feet. Her fingers tightened within his hold ever so slightly.

Two feet and he cast one last look up and down the long hallway.

One…

They raced up the stairs as if the guards were still behind them, falling through the door and collapsing on the other side in half relief, half surprise as if they'd not actually expected to get that far.

He watched as Star straightened and turned to look around at the room, wondering what she'd make of the large living space, lined with bookshelves on one side and a large television on the other. The sunken seating area was actually an illusion, the rest of the floor having been built up to allow for the cables and security measures fitted retrospectively to the ancient palace.

'Are we in someone's home?' she asked as she looked between the open-plan kitchenette that he couldn't remember using ever and the glass-fronted sliding doors that led to the balcony.

'It's okay, I know the owner,' he replied, watching her walk towards the view he woke up to every morning.

'I hope they'd be okay with this,' she said as she reached the partly opened door.

'They are,' he assured her, but his answer was lost to her as she slipped through the narrow gap and out onto the stone balcony.

He told himself he was giving her time. That it had nothing to do with having to get himself—who was he kidding?—his *libido* under control. He clenched his fists as if it would erase the feeling of her lip beneath his thumb, her between his arms, the ghost trace of her chest against his... Three years without sex might not kill a man, but one night without Star might just do it.

No. This was for her. He'd seen how devastated she'd looked. Whatever had happened, or not happened, this was about ensuring that she didn't leave with that look haunting her eyes. Instead, he reached for his phone, fired off a message to the palace staff asking for refreshments to be brought to his quarters, and another to Reza cancelling their meeting. He then purposefully put his phone on silent so as not to be subjected to the barrage of queries his oldest friend was sure to launch at him.

Clenching his jaw and ordering himself to behave, Khalif made his way out onto the balcony. He loved the large, deep green palms potted either side of the doors. The ornate, detailed carvings in the red stone balcony were almost as familiar to him as his reflection. Off to the left was a cream awning, under which were a table and chairs, but he knew that Star had seen none of it, her gaze instead glued to the whole of the city stretched out before her, beneath a sky that was turning the beautiful deep blue of early night and littered with stars more dazzling than any diamond.

'Burami?' she asked him without looking away from it.

'A very, *very* large part of it, yes.'

It was absolutely the height of insanity to bring a woman to his palace quarters. It was something the old Khalif had never done. Had he deprived himself of so much that he was at risk of recklessness? And then he remembered the look in her eyes as she'd sat on the steps and knew that he'd have done it all over again just to see her eyes sparkle.

He heard the soft click of his door, movement in the kitchen area that seemed to pass unnoticed by Star and the door closing once again. The last thing Khalif felt was hungry, but somehow it seemed fitting to serve Star food, when she had done the same for him. The memory of her basking in the sun sliced through him, competing with the dusk that surrounded them now and haunted his suite.

He retrieved the platter of food and pitcher of the delicious apricot drink he thought Star would enjoy and returned to the balcony, stopping mid-stride. Star was still looking out at the desert, but her shawl had come loose and now hung from her shoulders, leaving her hair…

Thick streams of long, lazily curling fire danced on the wind, a riot of golds, deep reds and every imaginable shade of umber, flooding his tongue with the taste of turmeric, paprika and cinnamon.

She had removed her denim jacket and the long-sleeved top slashed across her neck, leaving her collarbone and delicate neck exposed to his desire. The blue cotton, regal and powerful, strong and bright enough to stand beside the glory of her hair, made him think of an ancient astrological chart he'd once seen, created from the deepest of blues and golds, rich with circles, lines, arrows and stars, all working to prove some mystical assertion.

Mystical. That was what Star made him feel. And it hit him like a hammer, as if this moment was something they'd stolen from ancient gods. Something that was just for them.

Star felt him return to the balcony behind her. As if his presence had the power to pull at her like the tide. He was giving her the time she needed. And she *did* need it. She was in the private rooms of a palace looking out at the desert. She'd had to pinch herself *literally*, she thought as she rubbed the pink flesh on her forearm, to know that this wasn't a dream she'd conjured from her imagination.

She knew that she should feel danger, or at least a very real sense of concern. She barely knew Kal, but that felt wrong. She didn't feel as if he were a stranger. He was physically imposing, that was true, but, rather than making her scared, it made her *want*—want in a way that she'd only ever read about before. She had waited all her adult years to find someone who made her feel the things she'd only ever read about and she was leaving tomorrow.

Star might be very used to daydreams, but she wasn't naïve. She knew in reality that there was nothing past tomorrow for her, for them. But did that mean she should walk away from the possibility of what tonight held? She wanted to laugh at herself for being presumptuous, but… Her tongue ran over her lip, where his thumb had pressed so gently to such great effect. A tremor shivered over her skin and down her spine. Surely she wasn't the only one affected by this?

She turned, expecting to find him looking at her, having felt the burn of his gaze across her shoulders and back, but he was busy removing small plates from a tray, two glasses and a pitcher that was rich with condensation from the warm air, despite the dusk falling around them.

'If you'd like something alcoholic…?'

She smiled. 'No, thank you. I'm afraid the Soames women cannot hold their drink.' She reluctantly moved away from the balcony, fearing that she might search the rest of her life for something as beautiful as that view and never find it again.

She slipped behind the table so that she faced the cityscape edged by golden sand that looked like slashes of an abstract painting. He offered her a small glass of the *amar al din* she was going to miss terribly when she returned to England. Her mouth watered in expectation of the sweet, cooling apricot drink, but that was a mere shadow of the explosion of taste that hit her tongue when she drew it to her lips and she was helpless to prevent the moan of sheer delight that fell into the air between them.

'That is *so* good,' she praised unashamedly when she'd finished it. 'I'm going to have to learn how to make it.'

She chanced a look at Kal and veered back to the cityscape before she could be burned further by the heat in eyes heavy-lidded with desire. It scorched the air she breathed, jolted her heartbeat and pulsed and flared through her body.

By the time Star was ready to risk another glance at him, he had turned towards the desert, staring at the magnificent view as if it were his. Possessively. The way she wanted him to look at her. The way she'd thought, just for a moment, he had.

Blushing, she returned her gaze to the same view, wondering whether Catherine had ever seen it. Star had read over the journals Catherine had written while in Duratra, but she couldn't seem to make the descriptions from then fit with what surrounded her now.

'I wonder what this view would have looked like a hundred years ago,' she half whispered, her voice breaking on the words emerging from a throat half raw from need.

His reply was so long coming she'd begun to wonder whether he'd heard her.

'There was less metal, less chrome and glass, and it was a touch smaller. But one hundred years ago, Burami was still an impressive city.' She watched the way his throat worked as he swallowed, his eyes frowning once again at the view. 'The market you passed on the way to the palace has been there for nearly three hundred years. The skyline would have been not too dissimilar, the silhouette of the minaret and the cross, the turrets of the university. We've always had a mix of cultures, religions— mosques near churches, near synagogues, near temples...all from the very beginning.'

He spoke with a cultural pride that was unfamiliar to her, a sense of personal history she felt that she'd only just begun to experience herself.

'How long has your family been here?'

'Since around then.'

'It must be incredible—that sense of history, that sense of ancestry.'

'That's one way of looking at it. What about you?'

Star sighed. 'We've just discovered a grandfather on our mother's side.'

'And that is what has you upset?'

She resisted the urge to ask how he knew, but it must have been clear on her face. She'd never been very good at hiding her emotions.

'I… I have let my sisters down. My mother,' she said, hating the way that saying it out loud seemed to make it real.

'I know that feeling. With my brother. My father. I wasn't exactly their first choice,' he said before coming to an abrupt halt.

'Choice for what?'

She watched the way his jaw clenched in the darkness of the oncoming night.

'The head of the family business.'

'Really?' she asked, surprised. 'You'd be my choice.'

'You don't know me,' he replied darkly.

It was on the tip of her tongue to deny what he was saying. A half-forgotten song lyric hummed in her head about having loved someone for a thousand years… She shook her head, as if to free the words, but it only sent them scattering. Instead, she caught the words of one of her most loved books.

"It is not time or opportunity that is to determine intimacy; it is disposition alone. Seven years would be insufficient to make some peo-

ple acquainted with each other, and seven days are more than enough for others."'

He barked a laugh, not *at* her but as if *with* her, and she felt the appraisal in his eyes even as he made a joke of it. 'You just happen to have that to hand?'

'It's Austen. She should always be "to hand".'

'Oh, so you're one of those,' he teased.

'If by *"one of those"* you mean someone who reads romance then yes, I am,' she said with pride. 'And there's absolutely nothing wrong with that.'

He held his hands up in surrender. 'I believe you.'

'No, you're humouring me. That's a very different thing,' she said, not unkindly. 'It's very easy to be cynical and sharp-edged in this world. It's harder to have hope, to hold to romance and sentimentality, to allow the enjoyment of them and the sheer optimism, the faith of it all to sink deep into your bones.'

'Faith?'

'The conviction that love in whatever form conquers all.'

'And if I say I don't believe, does it knock a romance reader down dead?'

'No,' she replied, unable to turn to look at him with the smile on her face. 'But it seriously diminishes your chances of finding true love.'

There was a beat—of *something*. Something that passed his eyes and crossed his features before he barked out another laugh that had both traces of the humour she sensed in him but also the weight that pulled at him. And it was that weight she felt partly tied to, as if the deeper it plunged, the more it drew her with it.

She caught herself frowning, not because she was confused by her feelings—she knew what they were, knew that this attraction was something as unique as it was raw. She was confused as to what to do about it. Because, while she didn't need to know the why of it, Kal was holding back and Star just wasn't confident or experienced enough to call it out into the open.

But she didn't want to walk away from it either. She couldn't explain it. But she was sure, more sure than anything she'd ever felt, that if she walked away now, she'd never find this again. This feeling that sank into her skin and delved into her bones, that caught her by the throat and squeezed at her lungs. She wanted to gasp for air, she wanted to gasp for him. Just thinking about the way he made her feel had her pulse quickening, and something deep within her quivering.

The only place he'd ever touched her was the thumbprint he'd left on her bottom lip. She bit down once again, into the soft flesh as if…

'Stop,' he commanded.

'Stop what?' she asked, her words breathless, as she peered at him through the sensual haze that had descended like a fog. The muscle in his clenched jaw flared again and again, as if he was as reluctant as she was to voice this thing between them.

'Stop looking at me like *that*,' he ordered, and she wondered how she looked at him. She'd thought it was just her who experienced the flashover when their gazes met. The thought that he could feel something similar…

'Tell me,' she whispered, hoping he couldn't detect the begging in her tone, the tremor in her voice as she shuddered under the weight of her attraction to him.

'Tell you what?' he asked, his gaze still clinging to the horizon as if his life depended on it.

'What you see when I look at you like that.'

He bit out something in Arabic that sounded hot and heavy, half-prayer, half-curse. She saw him inhale, drawing oxygen deep into his lungs and expanding his chest, the breadth of it making her palms itch and her fingers tingle. He moved his gaze from the horizon to the table between them, as if having to work his way up to looking at her. And when his eyes finally cut across the space, up to her face to meet her eyes, she felt branded.

'It's not what I see but what I feel,' he said, his voice scraping over her nerves with wicked deliciousness. 'A heat that snags on a spark just begging to catch fire. I see a want so pure, so powerful, so...*naïve*...as if it would rush headlong into a burning forest and be happy to die in its blaze.' His eyes interrogated hers, leaving nothing unseen, unexamined. 'I see fuel for a flame that lies deep within me and a fire that I'm too tempted by to not get burned.'

His words caught her heart and drew it upwards into the night sky. Not one book had prepared her for how this felt.

'Which is why you should go,' he said, dragging his gaze from hers, but it was too late. The damage was done. 'You're leaving tomorrow,' he clarified to the question that had yet to leave her lips.

'I know,' she said simply.

'I can't follow you.'

'I didn't ask you to.' She knew that he belonged here as much as she was needed in Norfolk. But she also knew that she would never forgive herself if she walked away from the promise of this night. *One* night.

'Star, you're innocent. You are—'

'A virgin? Yes. I am. Does that mean I don't know what I want?' she replied.

'No, but that doesn't mean I can give you what you need.'

'Oh. Would you not treat me well?' she asked, not thinking for a second that he wouldn't.

'Of course I would.'

'Would you be selfish and only take what you wanted?' She couldn't even imagine it.

'No, I—'

'Would you not be very good?'

The question was a taunt and his response, 'Star...' was a growl on his lips, a warning and an incitement, a call to arms that she felt down to her core, setting her on fire, energising her in a way she could never have imagined.

'So you think I should leave and instead find someone who I'm less attracted to, who might not be good or treat me well and only be selfish in their wants?'

The thought burned the back of his throat and bruised his palms from clenching his fists too tightly. He couldn't argue with her logic. He had spent years cutting a swathe through Europe's most beautiful women and not a single one of them had caused this...arcane chemistry that burned the air between them—and his willpower to dust.

With his unseeing gaze still on the horizon, he felt her eyes like a brand against his skin, waiting for an answer, a response. His mouth ached to say the words, but he held them knowing he needed to be strong. He felt the subtle shift of her body as the fight left it and he closed his eyes, not wanting to see how giving up haunted her eyes.

Wordlessly she stood and approached the balcony as if the silhouette of his city contained answers that he was unable to give. She bowed her head and for a moment looked defeated. He wasn't arrogant enough to believe it was all him.

'I have let my sisters down.'

'You'd be my choice.'

'"It is not time or opportunity that is to determine intimacy..."'

Snippets from their conversation whispered once again in his ear, threatening to pull him under, the word 'intimacy' like a spell drawing him to her. Before his mind could catch up, his body had taken him to her.

He stood behind her, inches from her, his mind on all the reasons why giving in to this desire would be bad and his body itching to touch all the reasons why it wouldn't be. The glorious river of red had fallen over her shoulder, the delicate curve of her neck exposed. But it was when she moved her head slightly to the side, her pale skin gleaming in the light of the moon, willingly exposing her greatest vulnerability, surrendering to him completely, that he was lost.

He placed his hands against the stone balustrade either side of Star's, encircling her without yet touching her. The roar of blood in his veins, the pounding beat of his heart in his ears—something primal, elemental was taking over, and as he placed his lips against that stretch of the palest, smoothest skin he offered his first prayer in over three years.

The shudder that travelled through him rippled through her and he couldn't tell whether it was her legs shaking or his. He pressed his body into hers, leaning them both gently against the balcony, trapping her, holding her still. Her head fell back against his shoulder, her hair streaming over his forearm, offering him access to more of her. Rough stone was replaced by smooth skin as his hands left the balcony and swept around her petite body. He prised his eyes open to see the valley between breasts that were made to be held in his palms. He was torn, wanting to take this slow and wanting to take it all.

'Please,' she whispered.

And the leash on his restraint was lifted.

His hands swept over her breasts, palming the weight of them and feeling complete. His thumbs brushed her nipples into stiff peaks, ringing a shuddered moan that tightened Khalif's arousal. As if feeling it, Star arched back into his groin, pressing against the length of his erection until it was cradled against her bottom. Desire exploded on his tongue and he gently scraped his teeth against the muscle of her neck. She shivered again—and he felt it against his chest, his hands, his thighs and his calf muscles, questioning why they were still standing.

It seemed inconceivable to him that Star was a virgin and, despite feeling all kinds of selfish, he couldn't bring himself to stop. Unless she wanted him to.

'Star, you need to know that if you want me to stop—'

'Don't stop, please, I—'

He bent his head to hers so that his lips were against her ear. 'Nothing would make me stop. Not the sun falling from the sky, the desert freezing over, floods, locusts, or a third world war. Nothing would make me stop…but one word from you.'

'I don't need—'

'Star. At any point, do you understand? You can stop me at any point.'

CHAPTER FOUR

NOTHING WOULD MAKE me stop. Not the sun falling from the sky... Nothing...but one word from you.

Star couldn't deny that she had been nervous until he'd said those words. Words that had overflowed with the same need, want, *yearning* that she felt deep within her, and the *only* thing she was afraid of was him walking away.

She twisted in his arms, turning to face him, to look up into his eyes so that he knew. So that he believed her when she said, 'Yes. I understand.' She searched his face as if she was seeing it for the first time. Emboldened by his declaration, she was ready to stand in the path of his flame.

'Show me?' she asked, the weight of her desire making her voice shake.

He pulled his gaze from his observation of her face, her body, and dragged—reluctantly, it seemed—his eyes back to hers. 'Show you what?' he asked.

She bit her lip, trying to stop the smile that was ready to burst against her mouth. 'Just how good you are.'

She watched as the rich brown depths of his eyes were eclipsed by the pitch black of his pupils, his response marked in deep red slashes across his cheekbones. He claimed her then, passionately, possessively, his lips crushed against hers, his tongue slipping into her mouth, tangling with her as deeply and completely as she wanted him.

His hands drew her to him, the soft curves of her chest pressed against the hard ridges of his, but it wasn't enough. For either of them. He drew her up and she felt herself lifted from her tiptoes, her legs instinctively wrapping around his slender hips until she was above him, his neck bent back to kiss her, her hair streaming down around them, curtaining them within red velvet tendrils.

Her hands braced against his shoulders, revelling in the flex of his muscles beneath her fingertips, the power as he held her there, restrained and raw—and all for her. He looked up at her as if she were the most incredible thing he'd seen and she felt it. For the first time she really felt it.

He walked them back from the balcony and into the living area and a thought snagged at her mind. 'Is it okay? That we're here? That we…' She didn't quite know how to finish that sentence, but she read the understanding in his eyes.

'It is. This suite…it's mine.'

It was the first time she had seen him look worried, as if concerned what her reaction would be, or what questions she might ask. 'Okay,' she said simply, her faith and trust in him complete. He looked as if he were about to say something, to qualify or justify. 'It's okay,' she said again, before pressing a kiss to his mouth. Then another. And another. Lips brushed against lips until he opened beneath her and this time it was her tongue that led the dance, and raised a dragon within her. One that breathed fire and clawed skin. He had cast a spell over her and she felt transformed.

She lost herself to the feel of him beneath her, eyes drifting closed to savour the moment, and when they opened there was nothing in his gaze but lust. He turned and walked them through a doorway and into a room that faced the same balcony, the same view. Moonlight poured in through the glass doors, casting a silvery glow on a large bed with pure white sheets. Very slowly he drew her downward, his arms and hands cradling her back, so that she was ready when the back of her thighs hit the surprisingly high mattress. She looked up and saw the net canopy hanging from a hook in the ceiling placed at the centre of the bed and stretching out to the four corners. She felt like a princess and almost said as much, until she caught the look in Kal's eyes as he took her in, leaning back on her hands.

She watched as Kal pulled his shirt from the waist of his trousers, slowly undoing each button and revealing inch after inch of impeccable bronzed skin. Only once he had removed the shirt could her eyes roam as freely across his body as she'd wished.

He removed his trousers while she was distracted and on her next inhale she saw him standing before her, black briefs hugging his skin, revealing the contours of his body, the dip of his abs, the flare of his hip bones and the length of his arousal.

'I will stop at *any* time, Star.'

'I know. But thank you for saying it,' she replied sincerely and, no matter what happened that night, she was thankful. Thankful that she was sharing this with Kal.

He came over her on the bed and covered her with his body. It was only then that she realised she was shaking. But the moment his lips touched her skin that shaking became a shiver, became a well of need rising within her.

His hands slid beneath the hem of her top and lifted it over her head, casting the cotton aside as if the few seconds she was hidden from his sight were too much. Slipping the strap of her bra from her shoulder, he pressed kisses across her shoulder as he slipped his hands beneath her and flicked open the clasp. She gasped into the sudden freedom as he threw her pale pink bra from her body and the bed. The fire in Kal's eyes made her feel glorious as his palms swept up her thighs, rucking the jersey of her skirt into pleats that he bunched in his palms before tugging it gently over her hips and down her legs, from her ankles and onto the floor.

He trailed open-mouthed kisses down her throat, between breasts he cupped, the warmth of his palms reassuring, the thumbs against her nipples sensually unsettling. Her back arched involuntarily, pushing her body upwards against his, wanting more, harder, deeper.

His tongue teased the sensitive skin of her abdomen as his hands moved to her hips, hooking his fingers beneath the small band at her waist and drawing her knickers down, over her thighs, then her knees, gently pushing them away and making room for him between her legs. Her mind was overwhelmed with sensation and she was oblivious to thought or words, but a craving roared to life within her and she felt the echoes of the dragon once again.

She felt herself parted, exposed, but not vulnerable and she relished the groan of pure satisfaction from Kal, just before the world tilted on its axis as he pressed an open-mouthed kiss at her core. She arched against the wild streak of desire that almost lifted her from the bed, thankful for the anchor of his forearms holding her in place as a second sweep of his tongue stole her breath.

And she was lost. To pleasure, to sensation,

the sparks of fire racing through her blood-stream that she'd never known before. Kal had set them alight, making her glow from the inside, throb with a pulse of energy that powered both her sense of self and her need.

She heard herself begging for something she couldn't even name and gasped with sheer pleasure as his fingers joined his tongue. The unfamiliar feel of the stretch within her soon gave over to passion which gave over to frustration. It wasn't enough—she wanted *him*.

'Please, Kal,' she begged. 'Please.'

Kal reluctantly drew away from her. He had wanted to feel her come apart on his tongue, to show her the heights of pleasure before any kind of pain she might experience for her first time. But that was *his* want and this was about hers. His tongue swept out across his bottom lip to taste the raw honey and milk of her, not wanting to miss a single drop. She was exquisite, a man's final feast, and the thought that she would be the last thing on his mind before he gasped his dying breath stopped him still.

But then her hands reached for him, pulling gently at his shoulders, and he would have followed her anywhere. Leaning up over her, bracing himself on his forearms, he took in the pink path his rough hands and tongue had traced over such silky skin. The marks would be gone in the morning, but right now the primal animal satisfaction he felt at such a sight made it seem as if she were the royal and he were a beast. He traced his fingers over the outline of her hip, watching her shiver and buck beneath the lightest of touches, across the sweeping hollow of her waist, and tripped them over rib after rib after rib to reach the underside of a breast he couldn't resist cupping in his palm, the weight of it feeling like a lost pound of his own flesh. A missing part of him, one that he'd not known of until now.

He looked up at her face to find her watching him so intently that where he would have smiled, he couldn't. Could barely breathe for the sight of her.

'It may hurt, but I will take that pain away. That, I can give you,' he swore, hoping that she understood all the things that he could not give her. She nodded and he leaned over to his bedside table for a box of condoms that he'd never thought he'd need.

He retrieved the packet, tearing at the foil with his teeth, and felt the searing heat of her gaze as she watched him roll the latex over his length. He felt her shift on the mattress and looked up to find her leaning back on her forearms, her teeth punishing her bottom lip with a bite. He reached out to smooth away a rich red curl that had fallen forward and she leaned into the palm of his hand. Selfishly, he wanted to keep her there. Keep this moment. He could fool himself all he wanted but, while he would do *everything* in his power to make this special for her, he wanted this as much as she did.

'If it gets too much—'

'Then the sun would have fallen from the sky—' she returned his words to him '—the desert would have frozen and I would be myself no more.'

It sounded like a quote from one of her romances, but he didn't recognise it—it felt as if it were just for them. He kissed her back against the mattress and settled between her legs, relishing the way his body covered hers almost completely, fitting together like a puzzle piece.

His pulse began to race, awed by the trust

she had placed in him. He leashed himself with more control than he'd thought himself capable of as he cradled her face with his hands and pushed forward gently into her.

Her body tensed, as he knew it would, and she breathed in through the pain he could see she felt. He kissed her neck, the secret spot between her jaw and ear. 'It's okay, Star. Let it go. I've got you,' he whispered, holding himself still, impossibly still, until she was ready. Her deep inhalations pressed her chest into his as he dusted her skin with Arabic, words of comfort, of reassurance, promises that he'd be there to catch her when she fell. Star's body began to relax and he watched as her eyes opened, pain and shock replaced by wonder and desire once again. She nodded at his unspoken question and gently, and so, so slowly, he began to move.

He cursed. He prayed. He'd never felt anything like this. She was everywhere—around him, beneath him. His touch, his tongue, his taste was full of her and the air he breathed was laden with her. As her body undulated beneath him, he moved within her, their bodies joining together as if they were independent of thought and focused solely on pleasure.

Star strained towards him, her hand at the back of his neck pulling him down into a kiss that sent fire racing up from the base of his spine. A fine sheen dusted their skin, slippery and slick, sliding and tantalising, erotic sounds heating the air.

Star moaned into the kiss and he consumed it, the cries of her pleasure feeding his, bringing him closer and closer to orgasm. Each mewl of desire reached a higher pitch than the last and Khalif could tell she was on the brink. And he was torn between drawing out this singularly sublime moment and rushing them headlong into sheer bliss.

But then she tilted her hips downwards, drawing him even deeper within her, to press against a spot that saw Star explode beneath him, thrusting him headlong into an orgasm that stole his breath, his sight and his thought. The moon slipped behind the sun, the ocean poured away, and Khalif was completely and utterly spent.

When Khalif regained awareness it was to the feel of Star's fingers tracing swirls on his shoulders, her small hands slipping over his skin, as if stealing all the moments she could. Then he felt her lips tracing kisses down his spine, her body reaching over his as he had reached over her. He twisted beneath her and pulled her into a kiss as if the sand in their hourglass had already run dry.

Throughout the night they reached for each other almost endlessly and the sun was a curse on the horizon when Khalif finally made his way to the bathroom, running water from the tap—desperate to quench the thirst that hadn't quit even after the first taste of her. He was about to throw the protection they'd used in the bin when he noticed a small tear. And even had he closed his eyes to block out the image, his mind raced at the speed of light and all the while a voice screamed in his mind over and over and over again.

Pregnant.

Star could be pregnant. She could be carrying his child.

Star woke to the feeling of the sun streaming onto her skin, warming her and reigniting memories of the most incredible night of her life. She ran her hand over the sheets of Kal's bed, marvelling that it was his—the bed, the suite, the room in the palace. Sidestepping what that meant, she indulged in the belief that it had made what they'd shared a little more real, more meaningful than if they had been in a hotel room.

She was so glad that she had waited, that she had saved herself for him. He'd been so gentle, so generous, and her cheeks throbbed with blushes from the memory of what they had done the night before.

She turned onto her back, wondering where he was. Then, drawing the pale silk sheet around her, she made her way to the door, hearing the sound of voices beyond too late to stop her opening it.

The tableau that met her stopped her in her tracks. Khalif, dressed in suit trousers and a shirt, stood half turned towards her, his hands fisted at his thighs. A look of immense frustration was painted on his features for the second it took to register her standing in the doorway, before his face went blank. He was mid-conversation with another man, also suited, peering angrily at her through his glasses. A shift of weight drew her gaze to a uniformed security guard positioned in front of the door to the rest of the palace and finally a woman stood in the kitchen with a cup in both hands, gently blowing steam across the rim with a look of sympathy in her eyes.

Star shook her head as if trying to clear the image and pushed the door closed, hoping that the next time it was opened all these strangers would have gone and Kal would be there to tell her it was all a dream.

She was still standing there a minute later when he opened the door—through which she could still see the people staring at her.

'We have to talk,' Kal said, shutting the door behind him and walking forward.

'Mmm.' She wasn't so sure she wanted to talk but she was definitely sure she wanted a bit of breathing space between them so, for every step he took towards her, she took one back until the backs of her knees hit the mattress and she half sat, half fell on the mattress.

She clenched her jaw, trying to block everything out, even sound, but it was impossible as her eyes tracked Kal, pacing back and forth before her, his hands sweeping angrily through his hair. His lips, the perfect, sensual, powerful lips that had worshipped her last night, were bringing words Star could barely process into a room where they'd shared such incredible passion. Words that didn't make any sense at all.

In a daze, she tried to assemble what he'd said.

'I'm sorry, can you repeat that last bit? Just one more time.'

'I am Sheikh Khalif Al Azhar. First in line to the Duratrian throne.'

A sheikh. A prince.

He couldn't be.

But then she thought of the way he had looked to the horizon as if he owned it. The way that she now remembered his interaction with Wahed and the other guards, as if they had known each other. At how he had known his way around the palace.

How had she missed that?

She knew how. She'd been caught up in the romantic history of Hātem and the terrible tragedy of Crown Prince Faizan and his wife, and the loss that would be to their two small children. The tragedy had made the headlines of almost every international newspaper, with images of the twin girls being held by their grandparents and a stony-faced half shadowed brother she now knew was Khalif. There had been a subtle aspect of the exhibition that covered it—Samira's wedding dress, pictures, footage. The loss mourned by a nation had been handled well by the exhibition and there were references to an upcoming memorial to the short-lived ruler and his wife, but nothing had yet been confirmed.

He'd lied to her.

'Star,' he said, as if reading her thoughts in the widening of her eyes. 'You didn't recognise me and I…you were the first person to…'

There was a firm knock on the door.

'Not now,' he growled.

Star looked between the door and Kal. No. Not Kal any more. Khalif. His Royal Highness Sheikh Khalif Al Azhar. Hurt, embarrassment and shame flooded her as she realised that he had hidden who he was while she had been absolutely and completely herself. So focused on finding the necklace she hadn't been able to be anything but plain old Star Soames.

Rich and powerful. I am *impressed.*

Her shaking fingers pressed against her mouth. Oh, God. She'd said that.

It is not time or opportunity that is to determine intimacy.

She'd said that too. Had he laughed at her?

No. While she might not have known he was a prince, she *did* know him well enough that she could tell he hadn't laughed at her.

'But why all this?' she asked, gesturing to the door. 'Why tell me now? Did something happen?' she went on, wondering if it was fanciful to worry that perhaps a war had broken out, or that something had happened to a family member.

He came to sit beside her on the bed, their knees not quite touching, as if something more than his title had put a distance between them that hadn't been there the night before.

'This morning, I noticed that the protection we used had torn.'

She tried to look at him but he was facing straight ahead, as if confronting some unforeseen future head-on. She frowned. Torn protection? She couldn't quite see what he...

'You think I might be...'

'Pregnant.'

A baby.

Could she be?

A flood of pure bright light dipped and soared across her heart, her skin, her mind, before swooping to the floor and scattering like diamonds on marble.

This wasn't how she'd imagined finding out that she might be pregnant. She'd thought that there would be joy and a dizzying happiness as she shared the special moment with her husband, not a sense of confusion and disbelief and the father-to-be looking so…so *forbidding.*

'But it's highly unlikely, isn't it?' she asked him, looking for reassurance.

'That's not really going to work with my advisors.' His voice was heavy and grim in a way she'd not heard before.

'It doesn't have to,' she said, wondering why such a thing would be decided by committee. 'It only has to work with you.' She shrugged. 'I'll catch my flight home and when I can take a test I'll let you know what the results are and we can speak about it then.'

He smiled. It was a firm line of determination. 'There will be no *speaking about it then,* Star.'

She studied him until he finally turned and

locked his gaze on hers. 'Oh,' she said, feeling a tremble work its way down her spine.

'What?'

'The sheikh look. Does that actually work on your staff and subjects?' she asked, forcing herself to keep her tone light.

'Usually,' he said, his tone still cold enough to cut stone.

'I spend my days with thirty primary school children who throw much better tantrums than that.'

'That wasn't a tantrum,' he ground out.

'It was about to be,' she said, relishing the heat that had entered his voice. Heat she could deal with, cold…not so much.

'And that would be at Salisbury Primary?'

'Yes, how did you…?' Her words trailed off as she realised that if he *was* the Sheikh, if she *might* be pregnant, then of course his advisors would have looked into her background. As her heart slowly poked and prodded the idea that she might be pregnant, her mind ran like a stream over cobbles and stones. 'I always wondered what that would feel like,' she babbled. 'You know, in romances, when the hero does a "background check"? He usually gets something horribly wrong and so there's a big misunderstanding between them. I read this one—it was actually pretty funny—where...'

'Can we focus here, Star?'

'Of course,' she replied automatically, wondering how on earth she was supposed to focus when her thoughts had been picked up by the wind and scattered across the desert floor.

She looked up, finding one thread of thought to hold onto. 'Is it that bad?'

'That depends on whether you are pregnant with the heir to the throne of Duratra.'

Khalif left the bedroom while Star showered and dressed. He wished he could ignore the room full of people—the guard, Amin, Maya... No. He'd not ignore Maya. She had made herself as invisible as possible, but the subtle comfort she offered was everything to him right now. He could rely on her confidentiality even if she wasn't married to his best friend.

A best friend who would be calling him every shade of stupid for last night. And he'd be right. What had he been thinking? He'd been selfish. Completely and utterly selfish for wanting her, for acting on it, and now Star was going to pay the price.

This wasn't how it was supposed to be. He was supposed to get to grips with running the throne for a few years and then, after his thirtieth birthday, there would be discreet enquiries as to the availability of a suitable wife who wouldn't challenge him or interfere with his duty. And once the twins were of age, of course, the throne would return to them.

Years ago, he'd imagined something different, *someone* different, to wear his ring and have his children. But then he'd learned. Duty, the throne, family. It all came first.

But this? Star being possibly pregnant? He ran his hand through his hair, ignoring the uneasy glance his assistant sent his way as he stalked through the living area towards the balcony, stopping himself before stepping out onto it, remembering Star in his arms, hair streaming down around them. No one had ever affected him in such a way. Not even the one woman he had loved and lost.

He cursed out loud, uncaring of who heard him, his mind taking him to all the places he didn't want to be that morning.

Pregnant.

Star might be pregnant. And if she was? Then there was no doubt whatsoever. They would marry.

Showered and dressed in the previous day's slightly rumpled clothes, Star was looking out of the window when there was a gentle knock on the door.

The doctor. Star's pulse raced as she realised that she hadn't asked him what kind of examination or questions she was expected to submit to. Expecting a grim-faced old man, she was surprised when a pretty woman a little older than herself came through the door.

'Hello, Star, my name is Maya Mourad,' she said, introducing herself in English lightly flecked with an Arabic accent. Her headscarf was a pretty green and Star was a little distracted by it, which was why it took a moment to connect the name.

'Mourad, like the Prime Minister?'

'Yes, he is my husband,' Maya confirmed, her smile deep and full of the love of a happy wife. 'Khalif has explained that I would be seeing you?'

The gentle way about her was soothing to Star's edgy nerves. 'Perhaps "explained" might be a bit of an exaggeration.'

Maya nodded knowingly. 'I see. So, I am a family doctor,' she explained. 'A little like your GPs, but I specialise in women's health.'

'I didn't think that you could tell if I was pregnant so soon after...' Star's words were replaced by a fierce blush and suddenly she wanted her sisters. She didn't want to be here, no matter how nice Maya was. She should be talking to Skye and Summer about her first time, about how wonderful it was, not how she might be pregnant and how that meant she couldn't come home.

She could almost hear them now. Skye would immediately be making plans about prams and cradles, nappies and booties, Summer would turn to books and have all kinds of information on birthing styles, baby names and vitamins. Both of them would be completely supportive, with all the kind words of encouragement and soothing she could possibly need.

But there would be that silent *I told you so* in Skye and Summer's shared looks. They had expected her to get into trouble and, while they might not have forecasted just how big that trouble was…they'd clearly been right to worry.

'We can't tell whether you are pregnant yet,' Maya said, answering Star's half formed question from moments before. 'But first I want to see if you're okay. Then we'll talk about the options.'

'I won't have a termination.' The words were immediate and determined, natural and instinctive. They came from a place deep within her, and Star almost heard the growl of the dragon that Kal had called forth within her. 'I'm sorry, I—'

'No. It's good for you to know how you feel about this, even at this early stage,' Maya said, her gentle smile soothing a bit of the shock Star was beginning to feel. 'I meant options in terms of the kinds of tests we can do now, the tests you're *happy* to do now, and any medical information you feel comfortable giving me.'

'You mean giving Khalif?' Star asked, more curious than resentful.

'You are my patient. If there is anything you wish for me not to say, then you have my confidentiality.'

Star thought about it for a moment. 'No,' she

said finally and resolutely. 'I have nothing to hide.'

Maya smiled and gestured for her to sit. 'So let's start with the easiest question and then work back a little. When was your last period?'

CHAPTER FIVE

THE MOMENT MAYA emerged from his bedroom, Khalif demanded to know how Star was.

'She is fine,' Maya replied. 'Taking a moment, but she is—'

His assistant stood, snaring Maya's attention. 'Any medical conditions we should know
about? Family history of—'

'That's enough, Amin,' Khalif said.

'Your Highness, we need to know if there is
any—'

'*If* Star is pregnant, we will get to those kinds
of questions. Until then I will *not* invade her
privacy in such a way,' he warned.

Amin stared at Khalif until Star opened the
door to the bedroom and came out, with a smile
only he might be able to tell was nervous.

'As I told Star,' Maya said to the room, 'we
will need about eleven days before we can be
sure a pregnancy test will be completely accurate.'

'That's the day after the memorial event,' Amin said angrily as if somehow that was Star's fault too.

'Yes,' Maya confirmed as Khalif's head began to spin. Everything seemed to be converging on that one event.

'You can't miss it,' Amin said to Khalif.

'Why would you miss it?' Star asked Khalif in confusion and started a little at the glare his assistant sent her way. Khalif was about to say something when she turned to Amin. 'Are you okay?' she asked, peering at him. 'Do you need some water?'

Amin turned an indelicate shade of puce. Khalif couldn't tell whether Star had been purposely oblivious to Amin's obvious anger or simply unseeing of it.

'You cannot leave, Your Highness. There is still too much work to do—'

'Amin…' he warned.

'She can go,' Amin said, waving an arm in her direction as if she were a baggage to be passed around, 'but you are needed here.'

'Enough!' Khalif barked, his hand slicing through the air and any further objection his infuriating assistant might have. He was done. 'Out. Everyone. Now.'

Amin looked as shocked as if he'd just been told categorically that Santa Claus was real and moved only when the security guard in front of the door opened it and gestured to him to leave. Maya ducked her head—quite possibly concealing the ghost of a smile—but left and was followed by the security guard closing the door behind him.

'Did you want me to…?' Star's question fell short, probably at the look on his face which—if it was anywhere close to his feelings right now—would be a sight to behold. He resisted the urge to run his hands through his hair, aware of how much that would give away.

'Do you want a coffee?'

'If I *am* pregnant, probably not, no.'

'Right. Of course. Really? Already?'

Star shrugged her shoulders and stared at him as if he were an unexploded bomb. He certainly felt like one.

'Herbal tea would be lovely, if you have one.'

That he could do. He went to the kitchenette and retrieved one of the herbal teas he'd always kept for Samira.

His brain stumbled over her name as if, even mentally, he couldn't face it. He glared at the leafy infusion as if it were responsible for creating a link between Star and her at this specific moment.

Pulling himself together, he passed the cup under the heated water tap.

'I know you're a prince and everything, but if you don't know how to boil a kettle…'

He felt a smile soften the grim line of his lips and shifted to the side so that Star could see the steam coming from the boiling water.

'Ah… Fancy.'

'Very,' he confirmed. He turned and passed her the tea. 'How do you feel?'

'Not pregnant, if that's what you're wondering,' she said, gently blowing the steam from her tea across the rim of the cup. She looked up at him and shrugged. 'Kal— Your— Oh, please just tell me what to call you?' she pleaded lightly.

He smiled at her evident fluster. 'Kal when it's just you and me, Khalif in front of the people who just left the room, and Your Highness if there is ever anyone else present.'

* * *

If there is ever. Not *when*.

Star gripped the cup tighter to disguise the shaking of her hands caused by the realisation that he had no intention of introducing her to any more people than was strictly necessary. And while that hurt, could she blame him? She had only intended to share one magical night with him before returning to Norfolk. Something that now seemed impossible.

'I get the feeling you're not letting me on my flight,' she said.

'No.'

A dull thud hit her heart and blood rushed to her cheeks. Eleven days, Maya had said. She couldn't stay here for eleven days! Panic flooded her body, adrenaline effervescent in her blood. What about her mother? Every single minute she stayed with Khalif the necklace remained lost to them, as did the chance to save her mother.

She put down the hot tea before she could spill it and burn herself. 'I can't… I can't be here for eleven days, Kal,' she said, her voice almost a whisper.

'You won't be. In half an hour we'll head into the desert.'

'The desert?' Star asked before realising that he wouldn't want her somewhere she could be found by some unsuspecting staff or family member.

'We have a family residence in the desert.'

'Really?' Star frowned. She'd not heard or seen any reference to it in the exhibition. Maybe, just maybe... She couldn't tell whether the thread of hope winding around her heart at the possibility that she might find the necklace there was fanciful or fated. And then she was horrified at herself for thinking such a thing, for being opportunistic at this time, and her stomach began to hurt as much as her heart.

'I need to call my sisters.' They would know what to do, she thought, rubbing absently at her stomach—a move that Khalif's keen gaze homed in on.

'You can't tell them.'

Her eyes flew to his face.

'You can't,' he repeated. 'If news gets out then...'

'I trust my sisters.'

'I'm glad. But I don't.'

'You are cutting me off from a support that I need right now,' she warned.

'Then allow me to be that support.' His words were at odds with the grim determination on his features.

She turned away from him.

'Star.' She halted without looking back. 'If you are pregnant—'

'We'll cross that bridge when it comes to it,' she interrupted, not wanting to hear the rest of his declaration. Because she knew it would erase all the good that they had shared up to that point, all the moments of connection and how she'd felt *seen* by him.

'I need you to understand that while Duratra is a peaceful, inclusive and diverse country, even we balk at unmarried sheikhs with illegitimate heirs. Family is incredibly important to us. It comes first.'

'I appreciate that,' she said, still facing the door to the bedroom.

'Star. I need you to *understand* that if you are carrying my child, we *will* marry.'

No.

This wasn't how it was supposed to be. She was supposed to come to Duratra, find the necklace and return home to Norfolk, where they could find the jewels, sell the estate and get the treatment their mother needed.

Spinning to face him, 'But I can't be what you'd imagined as a wife?' she said.

'No. You're not.'

She pressed her teeth into her lip to stop the hot ache in her throat from escaping.

'But if you are carrying my child that won't matter.'

'So you'd marry me for the sake of our child?' she demanded.

'Yes.'

'But not love. You'd not *want* to marry me.' Star rubbed at her wrists, trying to soothe away the impression of shackles that her mother— that Catherine—had seen marriage as.

'No royal marries for love, Star.'

'That is very sad indeed.'

'It's just the way it is,' he said as if it were a tenet to live by. 'If you are pregnant, we will marry.'

Less than two hours later the Jeep jerked a little to the right as they skirted the base of another impossibly tall sand dune and he cursed.

Usually Khalif was a much better driver than this. He loved this drive. Not that he'd taken it in the last three years. No one had been back here since Faizan and Samira's accident—as if distance alone would help stave off their grief.

Khalif was hit by an overwhelming need to speak to his brother right now.

You're a fool, Faizan would have said.

And Samira would have looked at him with her large, deep brown eyes, accepting, understanding and hopeful that he'd found happiness at last.

He braced himself against the wave of loss that hit as inevitably as the tide. *That* was why he didn't like thinking of them. The pain that always followed was too much to bear.

He gripped the steering wheel and turned to check on Star. She had regained a little of the colour in her face. He resisted the urge to lift his sunglasses and rub his eyes, instead pushing forward with focused determination. As if the distance between them and the palace was something to be beaten into submission.

'I'm sorry about your mother's diagnosis,' he said. It had been burning a hole in his conscience since Maya had told him. He couldn't even begin to imagine what that must feel like.

'Thank you,' she said quietly.

'Is there anything that can be done?'

'We are working on it.'

Star stared at the rich yellow sand, rising and falling as if endless, silently praying for it to distract her. The 'family residence' in the desert was her last hope and she would turn it upside down if she had to.

Because if she didn't find the necklace and they couldn't save their mother then...then... she'd be alone. Her sisters loved her, but her mother *understood* her. And the awful shadow of loss she felt for the father she had never known would be *nothing* in comparison to what life would be like without her mother.

She cleared her throat against the aching burn and Khalif passed her a bottle of water. She refocused her gaze on the miles of golden sand and brilliant blue sky.

'How do you feel?'

'No more pregnant than I did an hour ago,' she said, the concern in his voice a kindness that softened her reply.

If you are carrying my child, we will marry.

It was only now that she might be pregnant that Star realised just how much she'd wanted to marry before having a child. It was in the way her heart quivered at the thought of her baby growing up to experience the same stares and whispers that she and her sisters had. An experience that Khalif had shared in his own way.

'But if I was,' she said hesitantly, picking up the threads of her answer, 'if I *was* pregnant, if we had a child, can you ensure that they wouldn't be judged, or excluded or…?'

'Star, look at me,' he said, removing his sunglasses. Only when she met his gaze did he continue. 'With every ounce of my being I would protect you and our child. Our family has an agreement with the press, both in Duratra and internationally, that protects our children from scrutiny until they turn eighteen. They attend a central city school until they decide whether they want to attend university. We can't protect them from everything, but we do our best.'

Star thought about that for a moment, not immune to the devotion and determination in Khalif's tone. She had grown up sure of her parents' love, even though her father had passed. Their love of her, love of each other, hadn't needed a marriage certificate. But her grandparents' behaviour had made her see through different eyes—ones that were hurt and had caused hurt. And she would never do that to her child.

'If I were pregnant, I would do whatever it took to protect them,' she said, finally turning back to him, knowing that he would understand what she meant.

'As would I.' His words felt like an oath and she felt the stirrings of the connection she'd been drawn to when they'd first met and something tight eased in her heart.

The sound of his phone ringing cut through the Jeep, but he put off answering it until Star returned to look out of the window.

Biting back a curse, he pressed the wireless earbud to his ear and pressed a button on the steering wheel to answer the call. 'Yes?' Khalif answered in Arabic.

'Wow. Okay. Nice to speak to you too,' came the sardonic response from Reza.

'I don't have much time. I'm on the way to Alhafa.'

'Really? Is that…wise?'

Khalif glanced across at Star. Nothing about his decisions had been wise since she'd come crashing into his life.

'There wasn't much choice.'

'The plans for the memorial are barely finalised, let alone—'

'I know, Reza. But what do you want me to do? Abbad will never be happy with the choice of memorial for his youngest daughter. We could have renamed the mountains and it wouldn't be compensation for his loss.'

'If that's what you're trying to achieve, Khalif, then…' Reza's voice trailed off, genuine concern evident.

He cursed. 'I don't know any more, Reza.'

'Well, at this rate, Amin might have a heart attack and be removed from your staff for medical reasons.'

'He's necessary.'

'He was necessary for Faizan. I'm not sure he's necessary for you.'

'Is that what you called me for? To berate me for messing up this memorial *and* my choice of employee?'

'Actually, I called to berate you for possibly

impregnating a British tourist, but sure, while we're at it, we might as well—'

'I'm hanging up now.'

'Khalif, it defeats the purpose if you tell me that you're—'

Khalif pulled the earbud from his ear and tossed it into the well near the gearbox, smiling. The moment of relief was, however, quickly dulled by the realisation that Reza was right.

If that's what you're trying to achieve...

'I am sorry,' Star said in the wake of the terminated phone call. He risked a glance towards her. 'For your loss,' she clarified.

He clenched his jaw, only capable of uttering the same two words she had given to his concern about her mother. 'Thank you.'

'Memorials are hard to choose,' she said, and he wondered if she had somehow understood the one-sided conversation. His anger escaped before his mind could catch up, his response a half growl, half scoff, questioning what she'd know about it, until he remembered the loss of her father.

'My father was cremated,' she said, her eyes ahead on the horizon, but clearly seeing some distant past. 'His ashes were scattered in the

Solent but Mum wanted me to have somewhere that I could go to, that I could visit if I wanted to. Somewhere just for me and him. She saved a little bit of his ashes for me, so that when I was old enough I could decide where that would be. I…' She trailed off, as if searching for the words. 'It was hard to decide. I didn't know him, I could barely remember him and I felt this…*pressure* to get it right, like I was being tested somehow on some instinctive connection I should have with the father I had never known.

'And then I realised that it wasn't about him, or Mum, or what people expected. This was for me.' She pressed a hand against her heart and his palm itched as if he felt the beat of her heart there. 'There's a forest near to where we live, and I spent days searching for the oldest tree. It's this beautiful old gnarled oak that's been there for hundreds of years. Mum, Skye and Summer came with me and we lit candles and I buried the little vial of ash in its roots so that he'd always be a part of the wood we both loved so much.'

Khalif remembered that she'd said her father was a carpenter and thought that it was perfect. It must have been a beautiful moment for her. For them. And he was struck by a spark of jealousy. Jealous of the privacy and intimacy of the moment.

'It's not that easy,' he said, his voice shockingly hoarse.

'Easy?' she asked, the tone to her voice making him realise how that had come out.

'I'm sorry, I didn't mean it like that. It's just that this memorial is not just for me, my nieces, my family, my country, but Samira's family, her country... It's...'

'Big.'

'Yes.'

She nodded. 'So all the more reason to find the one that feels *right*?'

He looked at her for a second longer than he needed to, causing the arousal he felt to sneak beneath his defences and grip him low and hard.

'So, tell me about this family residence,' she said, breaking the moment, a brightness to her tone that hadn't been there moments before. And if it felt just a little forced, he could understand why.

He sighed and cast his mind back through the

family history and legends of the old fortress. 'It's been there almost as long, if not longer than the city. It was originally a fortress between our land and the neighbouring countries, but it hasn't been used by the military since the fourteenth century. It was barely even used in the last few hundred years, but my father liked it and started to hold family gatherings there, especially since his friendship with His Majesty Sheikh Abbad.'

'Your sister-in-law's father? His country borders yours?'

'Yes. But, before my father, it was mainly known for being used for...'

He trailed off, as if not wanting to finish the sentence.

'For what?' she prodded.

'For the Sheikh's mistresses.'

'How fitting,' she replied drily.

'You are not a mistress,' he announced.

'No, I suppose being a mistress would require more than one night.'

Silence filled the Jeep as they both descended into a mix of memories and fantasies of what had been and what could be. Star wanted to bite her tongue and Khalif clenched the steering wheel.

They rounded the curve of a road that would have been invisible if he hadn't known where to look, and his pulse started to beat a little harder just as Star gasped in astonishment at the incredible medieval structure that was more beautiful to him than the city palace. The ochre stonework stood proudly against the bright blue sky, beside the rich forest-green slash of the palace gardens.

Despite its military exterior, inside smooth functionality gave way to intricate and ornate carved stone and corridors with rooms that opened up like Russian dolls, and mentally Khalif traced a path towards quarters almost as familiar to him as his own.

'Star, before we get to the residence—'

'That's not a residence, Kal. That's a palace.'

'Yes. Sorry, were you expecting—'

'Something smaller, perhaps? As implied by the word *residence*,' she teased. 'Sorry, you were saying…'

Khalif's stomach tightened, hating himself already for what he was about to say. 'Because of the situation, because we can't risk any word getting out, I have to request that you stay in your room for one hour in the morning and one hour in the evening.' She stared at him, those oceanic-blue eyes levelling him with their eerie calm. 'It is so that the staff can get what they need to do done, without seeing you. It's safer for you and them. No matter what happens, I don't want any hint of impropriety linked to either of our futures, no matter what they are.'

'Okay.'

'If you need anything at all, you can just leave a note in your room and they will provide it for you.'

'Okay,' she said again, forcing the word to her lips. Because the sharp sting of rejection was too familiar. Too tainted already with the feelings of shame and being unwanted. And right then she promised herself that if she was pregnant, her child would *never* feel the hurt of that.

He hadn't missed how quiet she'd been since his declaration. Yes, he trusted his staff implicitly and yes, they were all discreet. But he would never put them in a position that would leave them open to questions from the press, or worse—his father. It was vital that he kept them and Star apart. She would understand. One day.

He had shown her the gardens first because they truly were breathtaking. Thanks to the aquifer that fed both the nearby oasis and the palace, there was enough water for the lush greenery that filled the palace gardens and to allow the natural life in the surrounding areas to thrive.

It seemed to have a similar effect on Star as a rosy blush was brought back to features turned stark by the restrictions he had placed on her. He would have wanted to show her more, but he needed to get Star settled so that he could call his father and explain his sudden departure. He drew her back towards the interior of the palace the family affectionately called Al-hafa, escaping the searing heat of the desert sun the moment they passed through the doors. The thick outer walls of the palace, deep corridors and open courtyards worked to keep the internal temperature cool and manageable.

'This entire wing has the family suites,' he explained as he led her down the left-hand side of the palace.

'I don't want to take someone's room,' Star announced. It might have been the first thing she'd said since they'd left the Jeep.

'It's just us here.'

She nodded, keeping her head down.

'Thankfully, my father listened to my mother and had the suites fitted with en suite bathrooms when my nieces were born. She refused to have her granddaughters spending time in a military fortress with no decent plumbing.'

As he'd hoped, it drew a gentle laugh from Star and the sound tripped down his back.

'It didn't matter for you and your brother?'

'We were boys. It was different. It was good to toughen us up a little.'

Star looked towards a corridor shrouded in darkness. 'What's down there?'

'Nothing,' he said as icy fingers gripped his heart.

'But—'

'That area is off-limits.'

She turned back without a word and continued in the direction they'd been heading. His gaze was glued to her back because if he looked anywhere else he was terrified of the ghosts he'd see.

By the time they reached the room he'd had prepared for her, Khalif wanted to leave. To return to Burami. He should never have brought her here, where around every corner was a memory of his brother, of Samira. This was where he had first met her…and where he had last seen her. This was where he struggled the most to fit his feelings into a box called grief.

But it was the only place where he and Star would not be seen. And no one could find out about this. If she was pregnant, they'd deal with how and when the news of their engagement was delivered. If not…then they would go their separate ways and never see each other again.

No royal marries for love.

The words echoed in his mind as he watched her take in the room that would be hers for the next ten nights. She went straight to the balcony. The wooden screens had been pulled back to reveal the majesty of the desert. The bed was freshly made, the scent of jasmine hanging on the air from the beautiful blooms of fresh flowers in vases he'd not seen before. Her fingers trailed over her small suitcase as if in surprise and she turned to him, her hair swept over one shoulder, making him long to touch it.

'Your fairies have been at work.'

'I'm not sure how the staff would feel to be called that.'

'Well, they're invisible and do your bidding and don't you dare say you don't believe in fairies,' she warned, a slight tease to a tone that must cast spells over the children she taught.

'So that would make me Peter Pan?' he asked.

'And me Wendy,' she said, the teasing gone.

And suddenly he couldn't explain it, but his heart hurt at the thought of her returning home while he stayed in Neverland.

They both started when the sound of his phone cut through the moment.

'You can go anywhere you like—apart from that wing. I'll meet you here at seven and we can go for dinner.'

'Oh, taking me to the best restaurant in town?' she joked, as if his father's call wasn't important.

'It's *the* place to be,' he assured her with a quirk of his lips. And as he closed the door behind him, his smile flattened into a grim line and he flexed his hand from fist to open three times before retrieving the phone from his pocket.

This was not going to be fun.

Two hours later and the tension that had built across his shoulders and up his neck was as solid as concrete. The conversation with his father had gone about as well as any interaction they'd had in the last three years—terribly.

Have you forgotten your promise to Nadya and Nayla? You were supposed to spend the evening with them.

He had. He'd completely forgotten—but he couldn't reveal to his father why. Bitterly disappointed in himself, guilt and grief swirling thickly in his stomach, he promised his father he'd make it up to them.

But the words were over-familiar to them both. They had been a constant refrain in the weeks, months and first few years following his brother's death. Khalif had returned to Duratra and, even before the earth had settled on the coffins of his brother and sister-in-law, he had thrown himself into his duty. He'd sat up for nearly three straight nights, consuming every single piece of information needed. He'd made state calls, international calls, presenting himself as the first in line to the Duratrian throne. He'd handed over the running of an internationally successful business, stopped drinking, womanising, misbehaving and he'd worked. Hard. But he'd also hidden in that work. Hidden from his father, from his mother and most especially from Nadya and Nayla, who had been distraught not only at the loss of their parents, but also their uncle.

He couldn't face them. Any of them. It hurt too much. To see his own grief reflected in their eyes. He hadn't found solace with them, he'd found judgement, he'd found himself wanting.

Raza had intervened. They'd argued and fought until both were a little beaten and bruised, but Khalif had seen the truth of it. In the last year he'd been better, but he knew deep down he'd just been going through the motions.

Until a woman standing before a painting, with flame red hair, had caught his eye.

He almost growled as he stalked along the hallway towards the steam room in the lower level of the palace. His towel low on his hips and his bare feet slapping against the cool stone, diminishing some of the ire-fuelled heat that sparked across his skin.

He'd wanted one night. Just one. With a beautiful woman who made the weight of the crown lighter because it had been invisible to her. He'd wanted the taste of freedom she was unaware she had…and instead he'd quite possibly bound her to him for ever. Trapped her.

He banged the meaty side of his fist against the stone wall as he rounded the corner, welcoming the wet heat that was reaching out to him from the room beyond. He sent a prayer of thanks that Masoud knew him well enough to ensure the steam room was ready for his stay.

He pushed through the door and was hit by a bank of wet white air. He breathed in deeply, welcoming the mandarin and bergamot scented steam into his body, willing the heat to soak into his skin and relieve the stresses of an almost diabolical day.

He grounded himself, mentally drawing power up from deep beneath the ground, letting it fill his feet, his calf muscles, the base of his spine and up his back. He rolled out his powerful shoulders and flexed his neck from side to side. He just needed a moment. One to himself. He inhaled deeply again when he felt something brush past him.

Adrenaline and shock sliced through him as he reached out his hand and his fingers curled around a slender bicep.

'Star?' he asked, surprised and confused.

'Yes. It's me.' She sounded almost guilty. 'I don't want to intrude.'

He willed his heart to recover from the surprise of there being someone else in here, but his pulse didn't slow. Instead, his sight blocked by the steam, his other senses were heightened. He registered the silky sheen to her skin, his thumb smoothing away a drop of moisture, and found himself pulling her towards him. As he drew her closer and closer, she came through the thick vapour into soft focus. His eyes dropped to her chest, straining against a white towel pulled tight beneath her arms, rising and falling with the quickening of her breath and making him want to lose himself in the exquisite pleasure of her all over again and damn the consequences.

With one hand still wrapped around her slender bicep, he raised the other to cup her jaw. She leaned into his touch as if she craved it as much as he did. His thumb traced down her neck and tripped over a gold chain. He followed the loops of precious metal to the pendant that lay beneath her collarbone and stopped.

He took the pendant in his hand, holding it up to his inspection and clenched it in his palm, rocked by fury, shock and a grief as swift and as powerful as the harshest of desert storms.

'Where the hell did you get this?' he demanded.

CHAPTER SIX

THE MOMENT STAR winced as the necklace pulled against her skin, Khalif dropped his hold on the pendant and stepped away from her as if he'd been burned.

'It's mine,' she said past the pulse pounding in her throat.

'I don't believe you.'

The hairs on the back of her neck lifted.

'You recognise it?' she asked, shocked. While she had known that Hātem had kept the other necklace, she had never imagined that Khalif would be familiar with it.

'That necklace belongs to my family and has been with *my family* for over one hundred and fifty years,' he all but growled.

Despite his obvious anger, Star's heart soared. If Khalif recognised it, he knew it. And if he knew it, then perhaps she finally could hope to retrieve it.

'Not this one. Your family have protected its

sister necklace, but this one has been with *my* family for over one hundred and fifty years.'

He frowned, searching first her face and then the pendant as if it could reveal the truth of her words. He reached for the pendant again, but drew his hand back, a guilty red slash across his cheekbones.

Star held the pendant between them for him to inspect.

'There's a slight difference,' he said, turning the embellished gold design from side to side. 'As if it's the exact opposite.' There was something like wonder in his voice, until something dawned on him. 'I thought it was just a story,' he said, his eyes gazing over her shoulder on some distant memory.

Star placed her hand over his and brought the necklace back to her. 'I think we have much to talk about,' she said.

'Starting with why you came to Duratra.' His eyes were now firmly fixed on her, assessing her with an almost hostile gleam.

She opened her mouth to speak, but he shook his head.

'We should both be fully dressed for this conversation.'

* * *

All trace of the heavy sensuality that had built between them was now gone and in its wake was the horrible feeling that perhaps Star had an ulterior motive for being in Duratra. Perhaps even there had been some kind of plan behind their night together, a seduction maybe? But as Khalif gestured for her to leave the steam room before him, he knew that this was nothing more than paranoia and confusion.

It was simply the shock of seeing the necklace for the first time in three years. In line with their family's tradition, Samira had inherited the necklace on her marriage to Faizan. It had been on her that he'd last seen it. And where once dark skin had embraced and heated the gold, Star's pale skin and red hair brought the gold to life.

Star cast a look at him before she turned down the corridor that would take her to her room. He could barely look at her, the delicate shoulders, the trailing streams of red hair, the way that the thick white towel wrapped around her slender frame made her look vulnerable now. He pulled his gaze from her before he could once again catch sight of the necklace.

He had never wanted a drink more. But he hadn't touched a drop since Faizan died and he wasn't planning to start now. The last time he'd given into temptation...

Star had taken a quick shower, scrubbing the slick citrus-scented steam from her body as if it could rid her of both her unwanted desire for a man she might never again have and the discomfort she felt every time he saw the necklace.

There had been a moment when she'd felt hope. When she'd thought that perhaps she'd been meant to come to Duratra, to find not just the necklace but *him*.

Now she wasn't so sure.

She dressed in a loose-fitting T-shirt over an ankle-length skirt and left her feet bare. For some reason, she wanted to feel the ground beneath her feet—as if it might be the only thing she could be sure of.

When she knocked on his door a few minutes later she didn't hear him ask her to enter, but she was sure that he was there. Gently, she pushed open the door to the most incredible suite she'd ever seen.

She'd thought the room she was staying in was something from a fantasy. It was almost the entire size of the flat she shared with her sisters, and the impossibly large bed had mosquito nets that had become silks fit for a princess in her mind. The view of the desert was something she would take with her until her last breath. The detail of the carvings, the faded plaster and history pouring from every inch of the walls, was so different from the shabby neglect of the estate in Norfolk. It was as if it were full of pride and strength and love from every generation of this family that had ever stepped across the threshold.

She felt that and so much more as she ventured into Khalif's domain.

He was standing with his back to her, hands clasped behind him. Her eyes scanned the room, surreptitiously and quickly. It wasn't obvious wealth, though that was evidenced by the luxurious pieces of furniture, pristine despite their obvious age. By the gold, silver, precious metals and jewels that were scattered across tables, inlaid across tabletops, shelf-edges, doorframes. Everything was exquisite…everything was priceless.

It was that everything spoke of Khalif. The rich dark mahogany that was both weathered and strong, the hard edges and sharp angles opulent and eye-catching. The colours were masculine but there were hints of a playfulness that she sometimes felt he was capable of.

But in the centre of the wall that dominated the room was a shelf that was devoted to his family—photos, trinkets that one would collect, memories. *Family comes first.* It was a sentiment that she could both warm to and be warned by.

On the low slung table between them were trays of food, both sweet and savoury from what she could tell. Steam streamed from the spout of a large silver teapot and she told herself *that* was the cause of her mouth watering, not the power of the man in front of her. Her stomach was hungry, not clenched with desire and need. Her pulse was racing because she was unfit, not hoping for more of the man who had taken her innocence and left in its place a wanton woman whose sole focus was pleasure.

She took a step to close the distance between them and just over his shoulder was able to see what he was looking at that had him so absorbed.

It was a black and white picture of a family of four. Even if she hadn't seen pictures of him in the exhibition, Star would have recognised the good-looking man with the same jaw and nose as Khalif. Faizan had his arm around his two young daughters and was leaning into his wife, Samira, who was smiling at the camera as if there was nowhere else in the entire world she'd ever want to be.

Star's eyes were drawn to the gold necklace hanging just below the neckline of her silk top, almost exactly the same as the one Star had removed the moment she had returned to her suite.

He didn't flinch, noticing her presence, she felt it as if it were more of a tightening within him.

'She was very beautiful,' Star said, shocked by the sudden drop in temperature that followed her declaration.

'Tea?'

His question was such purposeful distraction, it was almost as if it were a challenge, or a warning. She nodded, but walked past him towards the view of the desert. Sand swirled in the distance, like her thoughts, shifting, scattering, only to be swept up by the air and thrown down elsewhere. Khalif, Samira, Faizan. Despite what her sisters might think, she wasn't so clueless as to go blundering into a clearly painful area for Khalif. But there was definitely something there.

She could see it as surely as she could see the sky begin to turn to that purple pre-dusk hue that always reminded her of lavender and salt. And home. She felt a sudden pang of homesickness she'd not yet experienced since arriving in Duratra. Suddenly she didn't want to know how Khalif's family had cared for the necklace, why Samira had worn it and how Star might be able to get it for herself.

She wished she'd never heard of the Soames diamonds, of the estate in Norfolk.

And then a swooping wave of guilt and horror overwhelmed her, knowing that without it her mother would have no hope for recovery. For her mother, for her sisters, she would face Khalif, explain it all and do whatever she had to in order to return to the UK with the key to the missing jewels, whether she was pregnant or not.

She went to sit on the long sofa opposite the chair Khalif had occupied. She took a deep breath and began. 'My grandfather died nearly a month ago.'

'I'm sorry to hear that,' he said, his formality clearly echoing the lack of emotion in her tone.

'We'd never met him. Mum had never spoken about him and I guess we just didn't ask.' There was so much she hadn't asked her mum, so much more she wanted to know. 'We were notified only because he had named us as... sort of beneficiaries of his will.'

'Sort of?'

Star shook her head from side to side. 'His will held a complicated stipulation. If we meet that stipulation, we will inherit his country estate in Norfolk. Which we could then sell.'

Realisation dawned in his tawny eyes. 'And pay for private treatment for your mother?'

Star nodded, breathing a sigh of relief that he understood. That he hadn't immediately assumed she and her sisters were simply out for money. 'It doesn't have to sell for the biggest

value—we have no idea what that would even
be. It just has to be enough.'

'Star, if you need—'

'We don't,' she said, cutting him off before he
could offer her anything. 'Because we're going
to meet the stipulation and sell the estate.'

*And Mum would get her treatment and be
fine.*

They had a plan, they would stick to it and
everything would be okay, she assured herself. It had become a mantra in the last few
weeks. A rhythm in her mind and her heart
like a prayer.

'So the stipulation…it has something to do
with the necklace?' he asked.

'What do you know of it?' she asked, hoping
that might give her some indication of where
to start.

'It's been in my family for over five genera-
tions and has been worn by the wife of every
Sheikh during that time.'

'Really?'

'Yes, why?'

It made her feel strange that Catherine's
necklace had been worn by the woman who'd
married Hātem. And by the wives that had fol-

lowed. Perhaps that was why she had not found a trace of it. She had been looking for it with the male heirs. And she suddenly felt a little foolish, remembering the words from the first part of the coded message her sister Summer had translated.

If you have discovered my message then I can assume two things: that you are female, because no man would wade through the private fripperies of my youth, and that you are clever, to have found the journals.

The pieces of Catherine's mystery had remained secret because they had been protected by women. As, even, had this piece.

'I might have been naïve to assume that Hātem would have kept it with him.'

Khalif shook his head. 'The men in our family do not wear jewellery.'

She nodded in understanding. 'And what do you know of where it came from?'

'I thought you were supposed to be telling me,' he said, half impatient, half grumble, his tone completely familiar to her from the little children she taught when they weren't given what they wanted easily.

'Humour me?' she asked.

He sighed and ran a hand absently through his hair. 'Honestly, even now it feels more like a fairy tale than reality or a part of family history. I used to tease Faizan about it when we were children.'

'About what?'

'That his wife would have to wear the *fairy tale* necklace.'

Star threw a hand-woven tapestry pillow at him without realising that the piece was from the seventeenth century and probably hadn't actually been touched for at least two.

He caught it one-handed and put it down with great care.

'I was a child,' he defended. 'Anyway, we knew that it had been worn by our mother, and our grandmother, and our great-grandmother and so on. Every generation was proud and protective of it, always ensuring that the first in line to the throne would present the necklace to his wife.'

Goosebumps pebbled on his skin and the hairs on the back of his neck lifted as he followed his thought to its natural conclusion.

'But you take it seriously now,' she said, unaware of his thoughts.

'Very,' he replied without hesitation. 'We were told that some day someone would come and claim the necklace. That it would be clear who they were and they would be given it without question or hesitation. Any more than that, I'm afraid I have no idea. My mother might know, but…' He shrugged, his mind still half on the thought that if Star was pregnant it might have found its way to her anyway. Either by becoming his wife, or it being returned to her, Star would end up wearing the same necklace as his grandmother, mother…and Samira.

'My great-great-great-grandmother came here,' Star said, causing Khalif to blink in surprise. 'In the late eighteen-hundreds she was travelling with her uncle as his wife's companion. They were passing through the Middle East and had come to Duratra to meet with His Majesty Sheikh Hātem Al Azhar to discuss Duratra becoming part of the British protectorate. Many other countries in the area had agreed, but Hātem had neither interest or need to do so.'

Khalif raised a sceptical eyebrow. 'And you

know this how?' She was right, but it was strange hearing her so certain of the thoughts and feelings of a man who had died over one hundred years before.

'Because Hātem and Catherine grew very close and she wrote about it in her diaries,' she stated, her large blue eyes shining up at him with nothing but sincerity.

'I don't—' He stopped short, his mind incapable of processing what Star was implying. 'This is not possible,' he declared.

Star looked down at the necklace in her hands as if trying to soften the blow of what she was implying. 'Catherine's uncle was called back to Egypt, but his wife refused to travel again so soon. According to Catherine, her aunt had a weak constitution, not suited to the climate, which irritated the husband she was angry with for bringing her to the Middle East in the first place.

'But Catherine was happy to stay behind. She loved it here. She begged Hātem to take her out on horseback so that she could explore as much of the desert as possible.'

'Star, this is all very fanciful but—'

'She spoke of an oasis. Which is what had

me confused,' Star said, not noticing the stillness that had come over him. 'I was confused at the palace in Burami because some of her descriptions didn't seem to fit. I just assumed that things had changed in the last hundred years. But when you showed me the gardens here, I realised...*this* is where Catherine met with Hātem. This is where she stayed with her aunt, and spent the night at the oasis with the crossed palms.'

Khalif's mind screeched to a halt. No one outside the family had visited the oasis. So there was no way that Star could have known about the crossed palms. A sudden memory of him and Faizan digging at the base of the huge ancient trees, convinced there was buried treasure to be found, filled his mind and heart, his ears echoing with the sounds of boys' laughter and the feel of sand against his skin.

'What do the diaries say of Hātem?' he ventured, half hoping she was being truthful and half still disbelieving.

'Quite a lot,' Star replied with a smile. 'That he'd seen what had happened in Egypt and the way it was being torn between Britain and the

Europeans, the impossible loan rates and finally the political coup. According to Catherine, Hātem insisted that Duratra had been fine without being under the British protectorate and would continue to be so. He'd been surprised when Catherine had agreed with him though.'

'Why did she?'

Star bit down on her lip, distracting him momentarily. 'Because she knew what it was like to live with a gun to her head.' She turned to look at the desert as if needing to gather her thoughts.

'When Hātem and Catherine returned from the oasis, it was to news that her father had died. Everything that Catherine had, all she had known, would be inherited by her cousin—a man who had made it clear he intended marriage. Would it surprise you to know that Hātem asked Catherine to marry him?'

'Yes,' Khalif barked. And then, 'No. At this point, Star, I don't think anything would surprise me,' he said, reaching for his tea to quench both his thirst and his wonder at all of this…information he'd never known about his ancestor.

'Catherine knew that he was betrothed to Alyah. She thought Alyah would be a good bride for Hātem.'

'Really?' Khalif asked, knowing, of course, that Hātem had married Alyah.

Star leaned towards him with one of the little leather journals she had brought with her gently held open and pointed to the top of one of the pages.

He will be happy with Alyah. Kind, loving and patient... We are too similar, too adventurous, too impatient. But he refuses to see that.

'What did she mean by that? That he refuses to see it?'

'Hātem didn't believe that Catherine had to return to England. She said, *Men think women know nothing of duty. Sometimes it is all we've ever known.* He just couldn't see why she wouldn't stay and they parted on not so great terms.'

'But if they left on such bad terms, how did Alyah end up with the necklace?' He felt like an impatient schoolboy, desperate to hear the end of the story.

'I thought this was fanciful and…?'

He cut her off mid-taunt with a glare.

'Really?' she demanded. 'Does that stare *really* work on your staff?'

'Yes!' he groused. 'Just not with you,' he said through only half reluctant laughter.

'Catherine wrote to Hātem when she got back to England. Her marriage to her cousin Anthony was much worse than she had expected. He was violent and verbally abusive. The journals really only continued for a few years after the marriage and then she had them packed away, so it's a little hard to say. But she'd reached out to ask a favour of Hātem. She hoped that he would make her a key that could be separated into two parts. One part was to be kept by her, and one to be kept by him, guarded until the day someone came to find it.'

'What is it the key to?'

'Catherine wanted somewhere safe to hide things from Anthony. Her diaries, pictures… and the one thing that Anthony wanted most— the Soames diamonds. Catherine left clues and coded messages in her journals for someone worthy of finding them, but the men in the Soames family dismissed or ignored the signs.

Ever since Anthony, the Soames men have been driven mad desperately searching for them.'

'Because none were worthy of it,' Khalif realised. 'So, the necklace is actually a key?'

'When the two are joined, yes. They will open the locked room marked on the map of the secret passageways that Skye found the day we…my last day in Burami,' Star stumbled.

Khalif was too caught up in the story to notice, only now making the connection between how down she had been and her desperate need to help her mother. 'That's why you were so sad? Your sister had found the map, but you hadn't found the key?' He nodded to himself. 'And with the diamonds…'

'If we find the diamonds we can inherit the entire estate and then sell it to fund Mum's treatment.'

'I imagine you could do a lot more than that.'

'We don't want anything more than that. Nor do we need it.'

It was said so simply, as if she was genuinely confused as to why they might want to have more than they needed.

'It's just that…' He tried to find the words to explain. 'It would seem that Catherine went to a lot of trouble to keep those diamonds safe for someone worthy to inherit. And to sell them for less than their value…'

'I think Catherine would understand our duty to our mother over the weight of the past,' she said with a finality and firmness that surprised him a little.

Khalif looked out to the balcony and the night sky beyond, his fingers rubbing at the slight stubble on his jaw and chin as he traced the stars with his gaze. He wondered if it was fanciful to think that the historic link between their families might account for the instant impact Star had made on him.

And then she shifted, her hair cascading over her shoulders, down her back and his gut clenched. No. That was all Star. So Hātem had taken Catherine to the oasis… He couldn't help but wonder whether Catherine was the reason Alhafa was known for hiding royal mistresses. Hātem and Alyah had made Burami their central residence and it had been that way ever since.

'What does it mean, Alhafa?'

His language on her tongue sounded soft and strange but utterly hypnotic. 'I suppose the closest translation in English would be The Edge. You can view the desert from every window and it often feels as if we're at the edge of the world.'

'It's truly beautiful.'

'My brother would have agreed with you. I...don't find it easy being back here,' he admitted. 'Nadya and Nayla loved this palace. Faizan was planning to move them here permanently. When they were younger the twins would run screaming down the corridors, terrifying the staff...' He couldn't help but smile at the memory, but it wobbled as he realised how much he'd cut himself off from them. 'Faizan taught them to swim in the pool, just like our father had taught us. It was where we...we met Samira. Her father's family came to visit one summer.' Samira would have been exactly the same age as the twins were now, the realisation catching him by surprise. 'On the first day, she climbed up the tree in the courtyard and refused to come down.'

'What did it take to bring her down?'

Me.

'Food,' he lied, the word burning his tongue.

'Speaking of which…it's getting late. I'm sorry that wasn't a proper meal, just snacks and—'

'It was perfect. I wasn't hugely hungry,' she said with a smile. 'Though I might be tomorrow,' she warned.

'Then tomorrow we will have a feast,' he assured her.

She stood, but appeared hesitant, worried almost.

'What is it?'

'Khalif, do you know where the necklace is?'

Her large blue eyes were wide with hope. For a selfish moment he wanted to deny that he did. He wanted to refuse her the legacy that was so clearly hers because the necklace was so entangled with his memories. A thread woven through his family that to unpick it, to remove it from them would make Samira the last wearer…

'Yes. I do,' he said gravely.

'Is it here? Can I see it?' For a moment he thought she might clasp his shirt, but instead her hands were entwined before her.

'Star, it's back in Burami, I'm sorry.' She bit her bottom lip again and the sight made him want to soothe away the punishment with his thumb. 'I will speak to my family, but I do believe you, and I believe that it belongs with you.'

'Thank you.'

He gestured for her to go before him and followed her out into the gently lit corridor, realising for the first time that her feet were bare. The sight of them had his fists clenching and he wrestled to get himself under control. He absolutely refused to believe that he had developed a foot fetish in the last twenty-four hours, but he couldn't deny the wicked bent to his thoughts.

He knew that she could feel it too. Hadn't missed the way that her shoulders had tightened, how she'd tilted her head just a little to the side, as she had done only the night before in Burami. He'd pressed his lips and tongue to that spot on her neck...

This time it was he that punished his lip with his teeth, hoping that the short sting would bring him back to his senses. Senses that were almost completely filled with her. She reached the doorway and turned, her hand against the wood, as if anchoring her in place, for which he was thankful. She looked up at him and he was instantly aware of how he towered over her, filled with memories of covering her completely with his body, her pheromones already making him recognise her as his.

She rose onto her tiptoes and he stilled, unsure as to whether he wanted to encourage her or not. Leaning in, she turned her head just slightly and pressed the simplest of kisses against his cheek and it held all the power of a tsunami. While he was trying to navigate his way through the swirling waves, she disappeared into her room and he was left in the dark, clenching his fists, feeling far too much.

CHAPTER SEVEN

KHALIF WOKE FROM a nightmare, heart pounding, skin sweat-soaked, his body tangled in the sheets. The bands of a tension headache pressed against his temple before he'd even opened his eyes, and the cords of his neck ached as if he'd roared his way through the night.

The phone by his bed lit up as it vibrated and he didn't need to check it to see that he had about thirty unread emails and probably at least eight missed calls from his father about the memorial.

He looked at the clock, guessing that it was early as the sun was yet to rise. Five thirty a.m. felt brutal after last night, but there was no way he was going back to bed. The conversations he'd had with Star had felt oppressive and he still hadn't shaken the weight of the past from his shoulders.

He got dressed, choosing loose trousers and shirt, and placed the *kufi* on his head before wrapping the *keffiyeh* into a turban, pressing his palms against the secure familiar material that felt as if it were keeping the pounding in his head contained.

He made his way down dark corridors, not quite ready to let go of his grief, of the images and memories of his brother...of Samira. Of the way she had looked at him just before she'd married his brother.

His heart flared as he stalked towards the stables, looking for his favourite horse. Mavia, a true queen like her namesake was regal, strong, proud and determined, and by far the best in his stable.

She greeted him like a jilted lover and he would have expected nothing less. He really shouldn't have been away from Alhafa for so long. But within moments she was nudging him with her head and demanding the affection he was always willing to give her.

He made short work of her saddle, itching to ride, and he launched himself into the desert just as the sun began to rise and the moon and stars to set. He raced them up a dune and out into the far reaches of the desert—his back to both the oasis, Alhafa and Burami.

He wanted nothing but sand and sky, no past, present or future, just the way his pulse beat to the rhythm set by Mavia. He ignored the sweat on his brow, the fire in his thighs and the ache in his soul as they crested the dune and soared down the other side.

But his mind refused to let up. Doubts, fears, shadows and ghosts rose up around him like a wave of sand before the storm. For three years he'd rode the pain, the grief, the guilt and anger at both Faizan and Samira for their choices, bearing it in silence and in secret. He'd tried to bend and shape himself away from the wanton playboy he'd been and into even half of the leader his brother would have been, and the *one* time he'd slipped, the one weakness he'd given into...

Star.

Her name was like a prayer and a curse.

Only she was the one who would fall fowl of it. That her freedom was the price of his selfishness was nothing short of a tragedy. Everything about her, the bright, effervescent positivity, the gentle soothing babble of words, her enthusiasm, her hope-filled romantic belief... he would have to watch all of those things be dimmed by royal duty and etiquette. He would have to see her denied the freedoms she so clearly took for granted. He would have to see her caged.

How would he ever bear the guilt of doing to her what had been done to him?

As he came to the top of the last dune before returning to the palace he twitched the reins, bringing Mavia to a halt.

He couldn't.

And in that moment, as the sun crested the horizon, he swore an oath that if Star wasn't pregnant he would let her go. No matter what, he would let her go for ever.

Star peered out of her door, holding her breath. Not seeing anyone, she stepped into the corridor and stopped to laugh at herself quietly. She felt like a naughty schoolgirl being caught sneaking out of school grounds. But the hour she'd been asked to stay in her room had come and gone, and she couldn't stay locked up in there any longer.

As she trailed a finger gently across the chalky feel of the corridor wall, she marvelled at how light she felt, knowing that soon she might have the necklace in her hands. Her heart felt as if it had swooped upwards last night and was still soaring high. She'd desperately wanted to call her sisters to let them know all that she had discovered. But the memory of how low she had felt when she'd thought she'd never find it...that shocking disappointment had rocked the ground beneath her feet and she couldn't do that to her sisters. She would wait until she had the necklace in her hands, rather than getting their hopes up.

Star turned right, unable to shake the feeling that she was alone, as if she could sense that Khalif wasn't in the palace.

The silence was rare for her. There was always noise at the school; even outside the classroom children ran down hallways and played in the grounds. There was noise from the busy road she lived on, in the flat she shared with her two sisters. And even when Summer was away at university, Skye was always there, keeping her on track and running like clockwork. Star wondered whether Skye had realised that she'd kept her company almost constantly since the day that Star had met her grandparents.

She wanted to shake that thought off, the low

ache she often felt when reminded of them, but there was something in the silence…something about it…that reminded her of Khalif. Not the Kal she had met, though there had been a reservation within him even then. But Khalif the Prince? The man she might have to marry? Unease swirled in her chest and she rubbed her sternum, trying to ease it. She didn't feel as if she knew Khalif as well as Kal who'd she'd spent one magical night with. Because there was hurt and anger that Khalif was holding onto and she couldn't shake the feeling that if she didn't confront it—*him*—then she might never know him completely.

Room after room showed furniture protected by large white sheets, window shutters closed against the damaging rays of the sun. There was not a speck of dust anywhere—unlike the estate in Norfolk. But, despite that, there was the same impenetrable sense of isolation and mourning.

The loss of Faizan and Samira was palpable; it felt as if it were forbidden to utter their names. But that kind of grief could be dangerous. Locked up tight, stoppered, it festered, it wounded, it spread like a poison… And that poison could do very real hurt and damage. She thought of the twin girls, wondered if they were allowed to express their grief, to talk about their parents as her mother had encouraged her to do. Throughout her childhood and into her teens, Star had opened up her feelings, so that difficult became easier and painful became loving. And while there was still an ache, low and constant, deep within her, it was not to be overcome but accepted as evidence of that connection, that love, between her and her father.

Star found her way to the corridor Khalif had specifically declared off-limits and, despite that, she turned down it anyway. There had been nothing particularly different about it yesterday, just a sense she'd had…until she'd seen his reaction.

Passing through a partially opened door, she came to a stop.

Unlike the others, this room looked as if it had only just been left. Drop cloths on the floor, half-painted walls, rollers stuck to trays with dried, cracked paint next to large tins with the same colours spoke of a half-finished decorating project. Moving further into the room, object by object she saw signs of a home, of life she'd not found elsewhere in the palace. A jumper had been thrown across the end of a sofa in the larger living space. Some nail polish on the side table. Toys scattered on the floor, waiting to be put away.

They were signs of a family.

Faizan and Samira's family. She turned back to the room where she'd seen the most decorating equipment and realised that it must have been the twins' room and an overwhelming cascade of sadness drenched her where she stood.

There was something so incredibly tragic about the half-finished rooms—as if Faizan and Samira's hopes for their children were only half fulfilled. It looked as if the decorators had stopped suddenly, midway through the day. Perhaps to the news of the shocking accident.

She looked at the two tiny beds, now far too small for the twin Princesses, and turned back into the living area, drawn to the warmth and the everydayness of the family photos on the tables and the book lying open at a page.

Star could understand why it had been left, but still…it was such a shame to keep Nadya and Nayla from what was supposed to have been their home, from what their parents had wanted for them. She frowned, looking at the colours chosen for the room, the sweet style of shelving, and she could almost make out how beautiful it would have looked, had it been finished.

She was about to turn back into the corridor when she felt the hairs on her neck lift.

'What are you doing in here?'

She turned to find him full of thunder, heavy dark curls of sweat-soaked hair slicked to his head, his chest heaving as if he'd run here from the desert. His white *thobe* open at the collar, as if he'd been interrupted in the midst of changing it. He looked like an Arabian Darcy having caught her trespassing, but there was no eager welcome in his gaze, no tentative hope in his demeanour. Instead he stood, refusing to cross the threshold, staring at her as if she'd committed a truly heinous crime.

'How dare you?'

Khalif was shaking with rage, grief and shock. He hadn't thought for a minute that Star would betray him in such a way. So when Masoud, awaiting his return in the stables, had informed him where Star was he hadn't believed him.

He tried desperately to keep his eyes only on Star but, not having been in these rooms for three years, his gaze devoured *everything*. It showed him things he wanted to see and things he didn't. Pictures of his brother and his daughters, himself and his nieces…of Samira. Memories hit him thick and fast and he would have sworn he could smell the perfume Samira used to wear drawing him, against his will, across the threshold.

'I was wondering why the memorial was so difficult for you. And then… I think I understand now,' Star said, her eyes watching his every move.

'You understand nothing,' he bit out angrily. Raw, exposed and vulnerable, he did not want to be here.

'I understand loss,' she said, not once breaking that serene stare of hers. 'Loss that has happened…loss that is yet to happen,' she said.

He hated that. He didn't want that for her.

'Whether it is in the past or the future, they are the same emotions, Kal. Grief, anger, resentment, devastation, helplessness. But this?'

She looked about the room. 'It's as if you all stopped breathing the moment they died. Do you even talk about them?'

'Of course we do,' he said, spinning away from her, hoping that she'd just stop.

'When was the last time you said their names out loud?'

'With you,' he growled.

'That's not what I mean, and you know it.'

'It's not important,' he said, unable to stop himself from peering through the doorway to the room that would have been for Nadya and Nayla.

I want the two beds facing each other, and the mosquito netting to be pink, and the nightlight to have stars so that it covers the ceiling with the night sky. It's going to be beautiful, Kal.

Samira had been the only other person to call him that.

'It might not be important to you. Or your parents, who must have many memories of Faizan and Samira's life—'

'Don't!'

In that instant he genuinely wasn't sure if it was because Star used her name, or because of what she was saying, but he really didn't want her to continue.

'It's important to Nadya and Nayla. It will be, if it's not already.'

'What's that supposed to mean?' he said, turning, her words ringing in his heart.

'It means that I know what it's like to grow up in the shadow of grief. I know what it's like to want to know who your parent was before they died. You want to know everything about them. Where they came from, what they were like at every birthday you reach. Whether you're like them, whether they would have liked who you are becoming, whether…whether they would have loved you.'

Everything hurt. For Nadya, Nayla, for Star… for himself.

'And if no one talks about them, it's like a denial. A denial that the person existed. And that makes it feel as if the ache in your heart has no real anchor, cutting you adrift in your grief.'

He opened his mouth to ask, but she pressed on before he could.

'And this?' she said, sweeping her arms out wide and spinning in a circle. 'This suite? This palace? It was going to be their *home*. It meant so much to Faizan and Samira that they wanted to *live* here, they wanted to decorate this suite and make it perfect for their children. It's clear from the photos, the memories, the plans…this was where their heart was and their children haven't been back, their family hasn't been back to it and it's just so sad.'

It was an accusation that cut him to the bone.

'We were trying to do what was best for them,' he defended.

'No. You were trying to do what was easiest.'

'Don't push me on this,' he warned, half growl, half plea.

'Why? Someone has to. You can't stay like this,' she warned. 'You're unhappy with the memorial plans—'

'But they're done!' he yelled, no longer caring what effect it caused. 'Three years on from the accident and at least it's done.'

'Really? Then why are you so dissatisfied with them? You keep changing things to fix it, but it's never going to work if you know in your heart it's wrong.'

'You don't know what you're talking about,' he said, slicing his hand through the air, trying to terminate the conversation.

'At least I'm talking. Really, Kal, is everyone around you so afraid of you that they refuse to tell you what they think?'

'Okay, Star, you tell me. What do you really think?'

'I think you're so afraid of whatever you feel guilty over that it's stopping you from feeling anything real about Faizan and Samira. And because of that you've somehow allowed the memorial to be something not even half worthy of their memory.'

He felt the blood drain from his face. He wanted to fight, to rage, to shout against what she was saying, but he couldn't.

Not even half worthy.

He felt sick. 'It's a disaster,' he admitted through the acidic taste of bile at the back of his throat. 'Everyone knows it. No one wants to admit it. But trying to find something that Samira's father wants, something that my parents would be happy with, not to mention my nieces...'

He felt the weight of her gaze on him, could almost hear the words.

That's not what I mean, and you know it.

He bit the inside of his cheek, torn between

wanting to explain everything and wanting to bury it all for ever.

'Samira was six when her family first visited, I was seven and Faizan was eight. We were inseparable, terrorising the palace staff, climbing trees, wreaking havoc…until Faizan had to start taking lessons to prepare for becoming ruler. Then it was just the two of us. It's lonely being royal. Even attending a central city school, it's not that easy to make friends who understand the presence of adult guards, or who don't want to take advantage of who you are or your position. Samira understood it. She understood the constraints of royal life. But where I found it difficult, she seemed to thrive on it. She wanted to use her position to do great things. She would tease me about shirking my responsibilities and I would tease her about taking on too much.'

He missed the sound of her laughter. The way that it had lightened his heart and soothed the ache he felt there. He'd never found it easy being royal, but Samira had borne it with grace and beauty.

'I'd always thought, hoped…' He'd hoped so much. 'Faizan was due to marry the daughter of an ambassador but she ran out just before the announcement, unable to take the weight of public scrutiny. The palace was in an uproar and Abbad… Abbad offered Samira as a replacement. And everyone agreed.'

Without telling him, they had all agreed. Even Samira. Khalif would never forget the moment he'd been told. The sheer incomprehension he'd felt until he'd seen it in her eyes. The sympathy, the silent apology. Even now he felt the wound deep in his heart throb and ache.

'Had you never told them how you felt about her?'

'What do you mean?' he asked.

'That you loved her.' Star's simple words left vibrations in the room that could have cracked the walls.

He could lie and tell her that he hadn't, but it would break something within him, and he wouldn't dishonour either Samira or Star like that.

'I didn't have to tell them,' he replied, like he'd not had to tell Star. 'I did love her—' the words were both bitter and sweet on his tongue '—but the moment she became engaged to Faizan—'

He shook his head, struggling to find the words to describe just how much he'd fought, he'd wrestled and cursed his feelings. 'After she had Nadya and Nayla, my feelings changed completely. Everything changed. She was different...a mother. She had two beautiful babies who were her sole purpose for being and...' Everything really *had* changed.

'It must have been incredibly difficult to watch Faizan and Samira marry,' Star observed.

'She wanted to marry Faizan,' he said, knowing the truth of it. 'She could see how much our parents wanted it. She knew him, *liked* him. He was...better—' Khalif breathed '—he was the better man.'

'He was a *different* man,' Star stated.

'You should have met him,' Khalif replied wryly.

She watched him walk further into the suite, as if somehow dredging up the memories had released the ties holding him back and she was glad. Glad that he'd spoken about Samira. Love should never be something that caused shame or hurt, even if deep down she forced herself to acknowledge a pinprick of jealousy. But it wasn't as much pain as it was sadness for him.

Because he must have felt so incredibly *betrayed*. His family couldn't have missed his feelings for Samira—if *she* could see them still now. She believed him when he said that his feelings had changed towards her when she had Nadya and Nayla. But even so…her heart ached for him and felt now more than ever that he needed this as much as the girls did. They all needed to come home. To where their hearts had once been.

She took a deep breath and crossed her fingers. 'I want to finish what they started.'

He stilled, as if he'd been instantly turned to stone.

'I want to help make this a home for Nadya and Nayla.'

'I'm really not sure about that,' he said, turning to face her. She could see the warring in his eyes.

'I think it would be good for them.'

He nodded reluctantly. 'I'm not sure what you're planning to do,' he said, looking around him as if he wouldn't have a clue where to start.

'That's okay. I have some ideas. Would you like to—?'

'No. Ask for whatever you need from the staff. Just leave the list in your room.'

When Star didn't appear for breakfast the next morning, he had his suspicions. When he reached his brother's suite she was finishing the white undercoat in the hallway that someone had started over three years ago. Her back was to him and every time she reached upward above her head the sleeveless vest she was wearing lifted and he could see a slash of pale skin between the top and the loose linen trousers she wore. And he turned away.

He found an excuse to be at that end of the corridor a few hours later and was surprised by the extent of work she'd achieved. This time he nearly crossed the threshold, but he didn't.

By the time dinner came around, Star looked happy but about to fall asleep in her food. She had tried to keep up with his questions.

'How are you today?' had been met with, *'I still don't feel pregnant,'* which had been delivered with a tired smile. He wondered whether he should just hire a decorator for Star to direct. Even Faizan and Samira had done that. His thoughts flowed with a little more ease

than he was used to and he realised then—that had been the first time that he'd thought about them naturally, without that sense of creeping guilt and ache that often accompanied such moments.

The next day he found Masoud hiding in the suite's corridor, looking as if he were about to have a heart attack, periodically peering around the door frame and spinning back to look to the heavens as if in prayer. Khalif was surprised. So far, the staff and Star had managed to stay out of each other's way.

Stepping as quietly as possible up to the man he'd known never to break a sweat under *any* circumstances, Khalif peered over Masoud's shoulder to see what had made him behave in such a way and nearly choked on his own shock.

He clamped his jaw shut firmly.

For there was Star, without a care in the world, humming away as she painted large brushstrokes of admittedly *very* expensive undercoat over a nine-hundred-year-old fresco. Masoud was actually fanning himself and looked almost on the verge of tears.

'We have more, Masoud,' he whispered, re-assuring himself as much as the older man.

'I know,' he replied mournfully. 'It's just that this one was particularly beautiful. I just didn't have the heart to tell her...' He trailed off. 'She's doing such a wonderful thing.'

Khalif could only nod, marvelling at the way the head of the palace staff was willing to sac-rifice the ancient fresco for Nadya and Nayla, and even for Star.

'I am a little worried about the drill bits, though.'

'Drill bits?' Khalif whispered harshly.

'She's asked for a drill and several sizes of masonry drill bits.' At this, Khalif could completely understand Masoud's concern. He winced himself at the thought of what she might do.

'We can fix whatever needs fixing...if it *needs* fixing,' he promised, hoping that he was right.

The next day, once again, Star had failed to appear for breakfast and this time Khalif took a small collection of pastries with him when he went to the suite he was beginning to think of as Nadya and Nayla's.

Through the door to what had once been the girls' room, he could see that Star was already painting and yet again her hair was worked up into a large woven cloth turban high on her head. She had finished the hallway and had worked her way around the first corner of the suite and if he wanted to see how she was getting on he would have to cross the threshold.

As if she had been waiting for him to do so, she turned and greeted him with such a beautiful smile that his heart missed a beat.

What would it be like to wake to her each morning?

Not to the blare of an alarm, the flick of the coffee machine or the imperious visage of his brother's acerbic assistant.

'Perfect timing,' she said, looking at him with a gleam in her eye.

'No. Nope,' he said, shaking his head and holding up the pastries.

She looked at the food he was carrying and her eyes rounded with pleasure. 'Thank you! I'm starving. And there's just this little spot...'

He looked over her shoulder to see the stepladder.

'Tell me you weren't just on that,' he demanded, the fury in his tone catching them both by surprise and he bit back a curse.

'Of course. How else was I supposed to—'

'*Khalas!* No. No more,' he said, slashing the air with his hand. 'I'm worried about the paint fumes, I can't trust you not to go up ladders, I'm sure that you'll be trying to move those beds soon enough—'

When her eyes grew wide, he clenched his jaw. 'What did you do?' he bit through clenched teeth.

'I dismantled them before I moved them,' she said, as if that would make it any better.

'How did you—?'

'Well, they're not exactly Ikea, but the principle was the same, and the Allen keys were here, so…'

'Why were Alan's keys here and what does he have to do with…?'

He trailed off because suddenly Star descended into musical peals of laughter. She was almost bent double and sweeping moisture from her eyes.

'I don't understand what is so funny,' he said, trying hard to keep hold of his anger. She made it too easy to breathe sometimes. Too hard not to laugh with her. And for the first time in three years he questioned why that was a bad thing.

'Just take the roller and get into that spot,' she ordered like a military general. He looked down at his clothes. 'Afraid of getting dirty?' she taunted.

'Well, you're clearly not.'

'No,' she said, smiling as she looked down at the splashes of paint across her trousers and forearms. 'They're just clothes that prove how much I'm enjoying myself.'

She had a spatter of paint on her cheek and he itched to smooth it from her skin, but didn't. Instead, he agreed to do the area she indicated, despite the fact that he was already late for a video conference with his staff.

Colour started to appear on the walls over the next few days and Star now had him completely bent to her will. When he'd asked how she knew about dismantling furniture or checking walls for electrics, let alone the mind-boggling range of fillers, sealants, sandpaper sheets and blocks, she'd said something about a man from her sister's job showing them how to fix certain issues in the flat. And when he'd drilled through the wall and taken out a chunk of plaster he'd been half terrified—not that he would have admitted it on pain of death. But she'd only laughed at him and told him that fixing mistakes was the best and only way to learn.

That evening, Star finally managed to get him to open up about the memorial, but instead of questioning his plans, she asked him more about Faizan and Samira. What they were like, what made them laugh, what made them angry. He was recounting a time when Samira had smoothed over ruffled feathers at an embassy ball, when he remembered the nickname they'd given her that night: *jisr*. Because she'd bridged the gap between ideas, people, countries.

'And what do Nadya and Nayla think?'

He looked at her. 'Think of what?'

'The memorial.'

'They're six years old.'

'Yes. Six—not three, not one. Six-year-olds can even generally feed themselves.'

He glared at her teasing, feeling angry and awkward.

She paused, the teasing tone melting away. 'No one asked them?'

He shook his head, not quite sure why he felt so ashamed.

What do Nadya and Nayla think?

It was now almost midnight and he couldn't get those words to stop spinning in his mind. He hated to think that he might have contributed to a sense that his nieces' grief was something to be denied, or ignored. As if his own, his parents' or the nation's grief was somehow more important than theirs. Unable to shake that sense of overwhelming guilt and shame, he knew that he *had* to return to Burami. He needed to see his nieces. And at the same time he just might be able to retrieve the necklace for Star. The need became so overwhelming, he felt as if demons were chasing at his heels. He had to leave—*now.*

CHAPTER EIGHT

THE FIRST TIME that Star had made a list of things she needed and left it in her room for the invisible staff to collect, she'd been surprised to find that it actually worked… That within twenty-four hours, forty-eight at the absolute most, her exact wishes were fulfilled. Out in the middle of the desert.

She tried to stay awake one night to see if she could hear the sounds of Jeeps or even helicopters bringing the materials she needed, but nothing. They just appeared as if by Christmas magic when she needed them. Which wasn't helping Star's determination not to live in her dream world any more. They were human staff, not fairy godmothers, and she was sure that the spontaneously appearing materials had more to do with Khalif being a prince than the staff having any magical powers.

The fact that Khalif was royalty still didn't feel real. Yes, he behaved like a prince and there were as many glimpses of spoilt stubbornness as there were of grief and loss, but in the last few days she'd felt as if they'd been talking. Really talking. Building something, so that perhaps if she was pregnant it might not be so terrible. That perhaps having a child with Khalif could be her own happy-ever-after?

After her morning shower, Star crossed to the living area, hoping to find the bronze gold paint she wanted to use for the finishing touches across the girls' bathroom ceiling, so when she first saw the note that had been thrust under the door she assumed it was from the staff, apologising for not being able to track it down.

She was already thinking of other ways to achieve the look she was hoping for when she caught sight of the scrawled K at the bottom and her heart leapt.

It was only because she was distracted, she told herself later, that the thought that it might be a love letter crept into her mind. That was where her mind had been so that when she opened the thick cartridge paper she had to read it over three times before she could make out the message.

Which essentially boiled down to a quick apology for having to return to Burami. He'd be back as soon as he could.

Unconsciously she rubbed at the ache in her chest, telling herself that she was silly to have got her hopes up. To be thankful for the reminder that although he was a prince he was made of flesh and blood, not ink and paper and imagination. This wasn't a fairy tale romance. He was important and had been called away, and it wasn't reasonable to expect that he could have woken her up to let her know.

She arrived in Nadya and Nayla's suite to assess what still needed to be done. The bathroom was beautiful. Star knew it was a silly thing to get excited over, but it really was. This was where she had seen the touches Samira had planned most, the bronze gold taps and the antique glass panels. It was a faded beauty, but regal. There was an enormous roll top bath, only marginally outmatched by a shower unit dotted with pale pink tiles that matched the soft natural plaster that ran through the entire palace. But it was the midnight-blue that called to her. The depth and richness of the paint that had been chosen by Samira seemed as endless as the night sky. And when the bronze gold paint arrived she would cover the ceiling in stars. Large, small and everything in between. She sighed, hoping that it would come soon.

Star left the bathroom and walked back into the central living area to the project she had enjoyed almost as much, knowing that she could work on this until the gold paint arrived. She had kept Khalif away from this part of the room, wanting it to be a surprise. Wanting to see the look on his face when he saw the tree. When the girls saw...

She swallowed. It was quite likely that she wouldn't be there when the girls saw all this. Her throat thickened and she blinked back the damp sheen in her eyes.

No matter. It wasn't about her. It was about them. And they would know and see how much love had gone into this. And knowing that their uncle had helped would make it even more special for them.

She ducked under the sheet protecting the special project from view and picked up her paintbrush, trying to lose herself in the rich browns sweeping up the wall. Despite Khalif's instruction, she *definitely* needed a ladder for this, but she had been very careful.

She only had this to finish, and the stars in the bathroom, which was a good thing because in four days they would be returning to Burami for the memorial and to find out if she were pregnant. After one test, she would know whether her life would irrevocably change or go back to how it had been before. For as close as she and Khalif had become in the last few days, she couldn't deny that he had not spoken of what would happen if she wasn't pregnant. And she couldn't shake the feeling that the answer was…nothing. Nothing would happen. She would return to Norfolk as if they had never met.

But, even if that were the case, she knew instinctively that her life would never be the same again. She felt changed. Not just by Khalif, but by Catherine, by Duratra, all of it. It was as if the desert had seeped into her skin and bones and was part of her now.

But, like Catherine, she also knew her duty waited for her back home. She would return to Norfolk with the necklace, they would find the Soames diamonds, sell the estate, her mother would get the treatment she needed and… And then…

For the first time in her life, the thought of returning to the flat she shared with her sisters, and the job she loved so much with the children…it just didn't seem as exciting as travelling through the desert, or seeing what else was out there in the wide world. Meeting so many different people, all with their own stories.

It struck her then that she hadn't spoken to either of her sisters for nearly a week. She knew she was avoiding them because she didn't want to lie to them about the necklace, or about where she was. But she missed them so much. She retrieved her phone and hit the call button, holding it to her ear with one hand while she painted a rich vein of muddy red upwards towards the ceiling.

But as the phone rang and rang she was transported back to a bus stop nearly ten years before. Cold, wet, she shivered even now. An automated voice announced that she had reached Summer's answering service and the tremor that tripped over her body had her hanging up without leaving a message.

Minutes had turned into hours at that bus

stop. She'd sat unseeing, facing the road as it rained, stopped and then rained again. Her mother and sisters hadn't come for her. And the entire time her grandparents' voices ran on a loop in her mind.

We want nothing to do with your mother or you. Do not ever come back here.

And that was when Star had realised that reality was a much harder, darker place than stories ever could be.

Khalif hadn't meant to stay overnight, not that he'd slept for more than three hours, or let his staff sleep much more. But he was anything but exhausted.

Star had been right. He should have spoken to Nadya and Nayla months ago. If his mother had been surprised when he'd asked to see his nieces, she didn't show it. And neither did they. They'd run to him as if he hadn't stood them up only days before, they'd run to him as if he hadn't retreated from them emotionally and physically in the last three years.

He'd spent hours playing with them, building forts from cushions and sheets draped over tables and chairs. He'd smuggled in *ma'amoul*, the semolina cookies that had been a favourite of Samira's, and *ghraybeh*, the shortbread that his brother had preferred. And as dusk had fallen and their bellies had filled with the sweet treats, he'd talked to Nadya and Nayla about their parents. He'd always imagined that they would find it sad and difficult but the moment he'd said their names the twins chatted away happily. And while it had taken a little while to get used to, time for his heart to get over the initial jolt of shock and unfamiliarity, the girls had launched into a list of the things they remembered about their parents as if they recited it every day.

Nadya had wanted birds, Nayla had wanted flowers, and Khalif had managed to sidestep World War Three by promising that the memorial would have both. He couldn't believe he'd forgotten how much Samira had loved birds. He had, in the way only adults could, assured himself that the twins couldn't make a contribution that he hadn't already thought of. He felt as if he were see-sawing between a sense of sadness, happiness, relief and regret for so much wasted time.

He'd gathered his team together and informed

them of the changes—the *big* changes—he wanted them to implement. He was done trying to please everyone else. There was no way that could be done. Trying to second-guess what his parents, Samira's father and the people of Duratra wanted had only served to dilute all previous ideas and he would not risk that again. And despite the concerned looks that crossed the table from one side to the other about the timeline they had to accomplish those plans, Khalif was finally completely happy with the memorial.

By the time he'd finished the briefing it had been too late, or rather too early in the morning to track down his mother, so he'd returned to his suite, crashed out on his bed fully clothed and woke a few hours later with a thumping headache. He'd showered, dressed in fresh clothes and was a second mouthful of espresso down when he'd watched his father's cavalcade leave the palace from his balcony. Khalif couldn't say for sure that he'd purposely missed connecting with his father, but it had made the visit easier. Because he knew instinctively that he could not stand before his father—his *King*—

and keep Star's possible pregnancy from him. Only when he knew for sure…

Unbidden, the image of himself holding a child—*his* child—left him winded. Because in all the scenarios that had run through his mind—the practicalities of what would need to happen were Star pregnant—he'd not allowed himself to think of what it would be like to hold his baby in his arms. A baby with Star's blue eyes and his dark skin. Someone who trusted and loved him implicitly, without question. The weight of that responsibility heavier than a crown or a country.

In that moment, Star's possible pregnancy morphed from something to be feared to something that he might actually want, might look forward to. And in his mind he saw Star, staring at him with the same trust and love and his heart turned.

His mother had sensed it when he'd sought her out. She'd asked if something had happened and he'd forced his thoughts away from Star herself and instead to the reason she had come to Duratra. When he'd finished explaining what he needed, his mother had seemed surprised and curious, but had done as he'd asked without question.

Now that he turned the last corner on the road to Alhafa, he wondered how Star had been in his absence.

Still not pregnant, he imagined her saying and couldn't help the smile that formed on his lips.

Entering the palace, he went straight to Nadya and Nayla's suite. A quick scan told him that she wasn't there. She wasn't in her rooms either and the tendril of concern that he'd been away too long began to root in his stomach. The palace felt empty. He quickened his pace and went straight to the staff area, hoping that they would know.

He knocked on Masoud's office door, surprised to find the man glaring up at him from behind his desk.

'Your Highness.'

Khalif frowned, the shortness of Masoud's tone unusually censorious.

'Have you seen Star?'

'I might have,' he said, looking down at the paperwork on his desk.

'Masoud.' His tone rich with warning, Khalif glared down at one of his most loyal employees, wondering when Star had enticed him over to her side.

'Sir, with all due respect—'

'Masoud, I'm noticing a distinct *lack* of that due respect,' Khalif prodded.

'You should never have left her alone like that, with no company and no word.'

'Where is she?'

'Have you looked for her?'

'Of course.'

'Have you seen the incredible things she's done in the Princesses' suite?'

'Of course,' he said, even though it was a lie. He hadn't had the chance to see it properly as he'd wanted to see *her*.

'Well, then. She is quite likely to be by the stables.'

Unused to being told off by his staff—other than Amin—he made his way towards the stables, hating the fact that Masoud was right. He turned the corner and immediately stepped back into the shadows. Star was with Mavia, stroking the animal's long neck even as the mare nudged for more.

Mavia never did that. Not for anyone other than himself. Not even for Samira. What kind of spell had Star cast over the palace, making everyone fall in…

His thoughts were cut short as Star looked up and straight at him and he felt a punch to his gut.

Although she'd hidden it behind a quick blink of her eyes, he'd seen it. The pain, the loneliness. The hurt. And in an instant he remembered. What it was like to be left behind. To be sidelined. And he'd done it to her without even a second thought. He'd been so lost in his own needs—his own desperate need to plan the memorial properly, to impress his father, the country—that he'd left her behind.

He emerged from the shadows, an apology already on his lips. 'I'm—'

'Did you find what you needed?' Star interrupted. She had chosen those words carefully. Because she didn't want the other words to rush out. Words that would make her sound needy, desperate…lonely. As if she couldn't be left by herself.

Only she couldn't. Not really. Every single

minute he'd been away had felt like torture. Her mind had delved into things that hurt, things she hadn't thought of for years and had no desire to think of now.

Perhaps her sisters had been right. She wasn't ready to do this on her own. Either of them would have had the necklace by now, returned to Norfolk, and they quite likely would have found the jewels. She should have stayed behind.

Would she have been as lonely in the estate in Norfolk? No. It was the pain of knowing that there were people she couldn't talk to. People she couldn't be seen by. People who, as kind and amazing as they had been to fulfil her requests each day, could deny they'd ever met her.

Shame. She'd felt shame.

Again.

'Ye—'

'I'm glad,' she said, spinning away before he could either finish the word or stop her.

Tears formed, blinding her to her path, and she dashed them from her eyes. Why couldn't she have cried *before* he'd returned? she asked herself. Why not at two in the morning when she'd not been able to sleep? Why not when the horrifying realisation had swept over her that she had filled her life with people and distractions to escape from the feeling of loneliness and shame that had scarred her when she'd visited her father's family.

'Star...'

Khalif's hand was heavy on her shoulder and he spun her round to face him.

'Who hurt you?' he asked, staring deep into her eyes.

'You did!'

He flinched, but as if he'd been braced for it. 'I know. And for that I'm sorry. But I meant... who hurt you *first*?'

She almost collapsed under the sudden ache in her stomach and heart—as if the years of pushing it down, desperately ignoring it had given the pain even more power over her.

She tried to pull out of his arms, but he wouldn't let go of her. He searched her eyes, and she let him see. She opened herself up to the hurt so that he would know and was overwhelmed by it too. He cursed and, just as her legs shook, he swept her up in his arms and she felt...protected.

She knew she should tell him to put her down, ask him where he was taking her. Instead she just let go, ignoring the tears seeping into his shirt, the way her throat ached as if she had been screaming. Perhaps she had been, just silently and for far too long.

She closed her eyes as he took her up stairs and down corridors, almost afraid to look. She didn't want to go back to her room. Didn't want him to just leave her there. A hysterical woman out of sight of his staff.

As she felt him push through a door, she inhaled the rich scent of sandalwood and lime that she associated with him and curled more tightly into his body, not embarrassed enough by her neediness to stop.

He bent beneath her and sat, and she couldn't help but tense as she expected to be offloaded, but it never happened. He continued to hold her to his chest, until her tears and breathing slowed. At some point she registered his chin resting on her head, neither heavy nor intrusive. She was encompassed by his arms, as if he'd wrapped himself around her completely, and in that moment she knew that he'd make the perfect father. Just holding her, allowing her to feel what she needed to feel. No questions—not yet anyway—no impatience or sense of frustration or distraction. As if his only purpose here was her. It was almost enough to start her tears again.

'My mum didn't hide my dad from me,' she began, for some reason not wanting him to have the wrong impression of her mother. 'She spoke about him. There were photos of him in the house and always stories—stories of how they'd met, fallen in love so quickly... She would show me the things he'd made from wood, tell me what he'd hoped for his future...for *my* future. So I always felt that he was a part of my life.'

She shrugged against his chest, her eyes unseeing of the room around her. Instead she had been transported back in time, to the little council house they'd lived in when she was younger.

'I thought that's what families were. Just children and parents. Skye didn't see much of her father after he remarried, and Summer's wasn't a part of our lives so... I didn't know to ask about grandparents, about my father's life outside of us, until school, really. That's when I became aware of grandparents. The older I got, the more I would wonder about my father's parents. What they could tell me about him. Who they were. Were they curious about me? Had they been looking for me? Mum was fairly tight-lipped about them. There had been an argument...but she wouldn't go into the details. She just shut the conversation down whenever it came to them.'

Star sniffed a little, pulling her shawl around her and tucking herself against his side as if to ward off what came next.

'By the time I was thirteen, I had convinced myself that there had been a tragic misunderstanding between my mum and his parents. I thought if I just went to see them then somehow they'd just...'

She let out a painful breath, expelling the hope she'd once felt into the room. She shook her head in wonder at her own naivety.

'That they'd just *know*, and we'd all hug each other, and my kind, grey-haired, soft grandparents would welcome my whole family with open arms. I imagined Christmases with stockings—because that's what I thought grandparents did—and perhaps even Sundays at a house with a garden. I'd decided that they had a tiny dachshund. It was called Bobbi and it was half blind and would constantly knock into things, but we would take care of it, me and my sisters, while my grandparents cooked in the kitchen with my mother.'

She huffed out a laugh then. 'I should really have known it was a fantasy, partly because Skye always did the cooking.'

Khalif felt his stomach tighten, instinctively knowing that this story did not end well.

'I'd found their address from some letters my father had written to my mother when he'd still been living with them. There wasn't a telephone number and maybe I didn't want one. It would spoil my plan. I'd saved up enough pocket money for the train ticket, worked out that if I ditched school, I could get the bus to the station and the train from there. I copied out the map from the computer at school. I even took some flowers. Who doesn't like flowers?'

The thought of thirteen-year-old Star with a bunch of flowers travelling to see these people he already didn't like did something to him.

'I was so surprised it worked. No one stopped me, or wanted to know what I was doing out of school. I thought I had been so clever. Then

I was standing in front of the red-painted door of number thirty-four College Road. I'd imagined blue, but I quite liked the red. It looked cheery,' she said.

Her voice was laced with a sarcasm he'd never heard from her before.

'I knocked, and the woman who answered looked *almost* like what I'd imagined. There were still traces of the marmalade colour hair she'd given to her son, but faded with streaks of white. Just like the way her eyes faded from an open, pleasant welcome to something almost like disdain. She called for her husband without taking her eyes off me. "I'm your granddaughter," I said. You see, I thought they hadn't realised. But she had. They did. They knew who I was.'

She took a deep breath. 'They said that they didn't have a granddaughter. They said that I was unchristian and unlawful because my parents had never married and they told me never to return.'

Khalif cursed under his breath, not that Star noticed. She seemed to be lost in her memories. 'What did you do?' He was half afraid to ask.

'I found a payphone and called home, but of

course my sisters were in school and Mum was away. I left a message asking Mum to come and get me and then I waited by the bus stop.' She shook her head again, the silken strands of her hair brushing against his shirt. 'I felt like I'd let her down,' she said, running her fingers across her lips.

'Who?' Khalif asked, trying to keep the consternation from his voice.

'My mum. I knew why my parents hadn't married. It wasn't because they didn't love each other, but because they did, and they didn't need a piece of paper to prove it. I felt like I'd betrayed that somehow by visiting these people.

'I didn't realise how long I'd been sat there but when a policeman found me it was dark. He explained a bus driver had seen me on his route and been worried. They finally managed to track Mum down and they drove me home.'

It was only when she'd seen her mum and sisters, rushing from the door of their little house and sweeping her up in their arms, that Star had let the tears fall. They'd surrounded her completely with hugs and love and held her while she sobbed, the force of it shaking each and every one of them.

'The only way I was able to stop crying was when Skye began to read me my favourite story. From that day on, almost every night for an entire year, after dinner we would all sit down in the sitting room and take it in turns to read stories of love, hope, happy ever afters.' Until the memories of that awful day at her grandparents' home were buried beneath *Pride and Prejudice, Little Women, Romeo and Juliet, North and South, Sense and Sensibility, Gone with the Wind...*

'Did it make things better?' he asked, the vibrations from his voice rumbling gently into the side of her body pressed against his.

She wanted to turn her lips to his chest, but instead was content with her cheek resting there.

'It did. Losing myself in romance and happy endings was a much better thing than to lose myself in sadness, hurt and shame.'

She yawned, utterly spent and exhausted. Both the emotions of the last couple of days and the work she'd put in on the suite had drained her completely.

'Thank you,' she said, looking up at him, still encircled in his arms. 'Thank you for just listening.'

'Of course.'

He'd been about to say *Any time*, but he couldn't say it and know it might not be true. 'Shall I take you back to your room?'

She looked almost on the verge of asking a question before she seemed to think better of it, smiled, and said that she knew the way.

Long after she left, he sat in the room with her memories vivid in his imagination. To be so rejected by family was completely alien to him. He might have had a difficult relationship with his parents, but they would never cut him from their lives. They hadn't when he'd run wild through Europe and they wouldn't even if they discovered Star was carrying his child and that he would be marrying her.

He stalked the halls of the palace, returning to the suite that Star had been so consumed by. He knew that it would affect him, being in what had once been his brother's quarters, and he marched towards them, braced and ready for a fight—albeit an emotional one.

First, he opened the door to the bathroom. It

had been days since he'd seen it and the breath left his lungs in surprise. All over the ceiling and down the parts of the walls that weren't covered in antique mirrored glass or the shower was an incredible night sky. A deep blue paint was interspersed with thousands of stars, ranging from the smallest dot to an intricate eight-pointed star the size of his palm. It gave the room an infinite depth and he felt as if he were standing in the middle of the cosmos. He knew that it had nothing to do with ego and everything to do with fully realising Samira's dream, and in that moment he knew he'd never forget Star's kindness as long as he lived.

He was reluctant to leave the space, but he was equally curious about what lay beneath the drop cloth covering a large area of the living space wall. His hand shook a little as he pulled it away, as if he sensed that whatever it was would be profound, but as the cloth fell away he had to cover his mouth with his hand to stop his shock from escaping into the room.

A tree wound its way up from the floor to the ceiling. Branches covered the length of the wall, the texture and detail of the bark making him want to reach out and touch it. It was only as he got closer that he saw little hand and foot holds drilled into the walls.

The girls would be able to climb it, just like Samira had climbed the tree in the palace garden. Stepping up to the wall, he felt the floor beneath his feet change to a soft mat that would protect them if they fell. Star had thought of everything. He shook his head in wonder.

'I hope you can see this, brother,' he whispered out loud. 'Samira, I know how much this would mean to you.'

Now it was up to Khalif to try and repair some of the hurt he'd caused and it came to him instantly, knowing the rightness of it by how his chest filled with excitement and his pulse pounded.

He knew just the way.

CHAPTER NINE

STAR GENTLY PADDED down the corridor to the dining room she'd been shown on that first day and never used. She hugged the midnight-blue silk kimono around her, still feeling a little vulnerable from her conversation with Khalif the day before.

'No, that will take too long,' she heard Khalif say before she'd entered the room. The smell of cardamom tea made her mouth water and the sweet pastries she was going to have to learn how to make had her stomach grumbling.

'It will have to be the Jeep… Yes… I don't care about the expense, it's worth it,' he growled. The moment he saw her in the doorway, he ended the call and put his phone on the table.

'Was that Amin?' she asked, coming into the room and sitting down where her place had been set. He poured her a cup of tea as she took a few pastries—she couldn't say which ones because she'd become lost in the way that his powerful hands gripped the thin silver arm of the teapot, and then the tiny porcelain handle of the cup.

She blushed when he actually had to say her name to get her to take the cup he was offering her.

'Yes,' he said. When she looked up at him he frowned. 'It was Amin,' he clarified.

Oh, good God, she had to get a grip of herself.

'Why did you ask?'

'You always get that tone in your voice when you speak to him,' she replied, inhaling the scent of the aromatic tea that tasted so much better here than it ever had in England.

'What tone?'

'Mmm…that *I-don't-care-what-you-think-just-do-it* tone.'

The look on his face told her that her impression had hit home.

'I don't know what you mean,' he evaded.

'Yes, you do. He irritates you,' she stated easily.

'Because he judges me,' Khalif growled.

'Probably because you're clearly irritated

with him,' she replied, unable to help the smile pulling at her lips. 'You should either make peace with him or let him go.'

'And that is your professional opinion?'

'Absolutely. If you don't want it to descend into playground taunts of "He started it".'

Star could have sworn she heard him say, *But he did*, under his breath, but by the time she looked up at him he was furiously studying a mark on the table.

'How do you feel today?'

'*Still* not pregnant.'

He smiled, and her heart eased a little.

'I… I spoke to my sisters last night.' She hated the way that his body tensed, but she was thankful that he waited to hear what she had to say. 'I told them only that I might be able to get the necklace.'

'What did they say?'

'They are very happy.' It wasn't exactly a lie. They had been happy, or at least relieved. Star had intended to wait until she had the necklace in her possession, but she'd felt awkward keeping the news of it a secret. So she had told Summer that she knew where it was and hoped to have it soon. Star would have sworn she'd felt her sister's sigh against her skin as if it had whooshed through the phone speaker. Summer had mentioned something about making the meeting with the buyer easier and had then asked some bland questions about Burami, clearly forgetting that Star was now in the desert. It was a bit unlike her. Or had been unlike her three months ago…but ever since she'd returned from her mid-term holiday there had been something almost distracted about her, even though she'd denied it every time Skye or Star had asked her about it.

'And actually, Skye is engaged,' Star announced, thinking of the later conversation with her older sister.

'Congratulations. What's he like?'

'I have *no* idea. I've never met him,' she replied as Khalif blinked in surprise. 'But she's happy, I can tell.' And Skye really had been, happier than Star had ever heard her. It had been strange to hear Skye shine with the romance of her thrilling Costa Rican adventure.

It wasn't that Star wasn't happy for her, it was just that… She rubbed at her sternum, hoping to ease the tightness there. Was she jealous? Star looked at Khalif. Here she was, in the desert with a gorgeous sheikh, literally on a treasure hunt, and while it could look like the perfect romance for all the world, beneath it all, she was only here because she *might* be pregnant.

But as the days had worn on, and as Star grew closer and closer to the man she'd first met and merged that with the complexities of the man before her, as she felt her heart slowly spread and stretch, she began to suspect that she wasn't pregnant and could no longer ignore her fear that she didn't mean to him what he had come to mean to her.

'That's good, right?' Khalif asked, looking at her as if he were worried about her.

The tea nearly jerked over the rim and she had to place the delicate cup down before she lost even more of it. She knew that he was not speaking about her thoughts of him, but his words had still cut through her.

'That she's happy?' he clarified.

'Yes. Yes, of course,' Star replied, forcing a little pastry into her mouth before she could make things worse.

'Eat up,' he pressed. 'We have places to be.'

'Do we?' This really was a confusing morning. 'Where are we going? Don't we have to be back in Burami tomorrow?'

'Yes. But, in the meantime, you're being kidnapped by a handsome prince.'

Her heart soared, loving the way he'd just teased her. 'Oh, really? Where is he?' she asked, looking around the room.

'Funny,' he groused. 'Meet me by the stables. And dress comfortably.'

He probably should have asked her whether she knew how to ride *before* he'd made his plans, but the excitement and determination that had shone in her eyes was worth it. Mavia was so completely under Star's spell that he'd almost had to stop the mare from lowering to the ground for Star to mount.

If he wasn't careful, he would not have any subjects left in the country because they'd have all sworn allegiance to her.

Star had dressed as he'd asked. A long-sleeved white top and cream linen trousers were protected by a pale gold pashmina that compared unfavourably to the rich red ropes of hair that curled down her back.

But it was her smile that truly shone.

By the time he had Star on Mavia in front of him, his pulse was ready to burst. His horse didn't even complain once at the unusual extra weight, instead flicking a gaze at him from her bent head as if to demand what he was waiting for.

In truth, he was waiting to regain control of his body. He'd not counted on the way that having Star in between his legs and against his chest, or the way his arms felt wrapped around her would affect him.

She hadn't asked him a single question, he thought as he flicked Mavia's reins. She launched from the stables as if as desperate to show Star the magical wonders of the desert as he. Star's trust in him was complete. As complete as it had been the night they had spent together. It made him feel like…a king.

As Mavia galloped beneath them he relished the feeling of having Star so close, and he loosened his hold on the reins, his horse knowing their destination, having made this journey more than a thousand times, even if not in the last three years.

He cast his gaze outwards and breathed deep. He felt alive here. The stretches of endless desert a mirage, a trick she played on the weary traveller, to test their mettle, to see their true worth. There were no lies in the desert. She may not have been cruel or loving, but she was most definitely capricious.

In the back of his mind he heard his brother's laugh, urging him on, faster and faster, and it merged with the laugh from Star. He felt it in his heart, surrounded by adrenaline, excitement and all the things he hadn't felt for so long. He could feel it. The rightness of coming here. As if he had always been meant to bring her to this place.

They were so nearly there and Mavia knew it too because she found a sudden spurt of energy. They crested a dune, trails of sand billowing in their wake for no one to see, and at the pinnacle Mavia came to a stop of her own volition as if just as awed by the sight as the humans she carried. Khalif might have known every single inch of this view, but it still struck him as something incredible and precious, known only by a rare few.

He cast his eyes deep into the valley, over the large canvas tent nestled close to the trees that lined the small lake in the middle of the basin and in the distance he looked up to see the palms Star's ancestor had written of.

Star's mouth had dropped open. Her eyes raced across the image before her, sure that it was a dream. A desert mirage. But it wasn't. She could feel the heat of Khalif behind her and the pounding of Mavia's heart beneath her.

At the mouth of the tent, rich, dark red woven rugs stretched out before a large fire pit—one that was already in full flame. Golden glints and bursts of red hinted at sequin-encrusted cushions and rich deep turquoise silks covered the sand. A low-slung table with a dazzling array of drinks and food were kept cool and contained in a glass-fronted fridge. She was sure there must have been a generator somewhere discreet, but she couldn't see it. Nothing spoiled the fantasy.

The richness of what lay in front of her was almost too much to bear, so her eyes drifted to the far side of the crystal-blue water nestled within lush green vegetation to where she saw two palms crossed at the base to form an X.

Her heart missed a beat and she gasped.

She didn't dare turn around because if she

looked at Khalif now, he'd know. He'd know
that she'd fallen in love with him. And there,
wrapped in his arms, his hands loosely holding the reins, and half convinced that he would
be able to feel the beat of her heart, she almost
started to shake.

Khalif urged the horse forward and they jos-
tled from side to side with the horse's uneven
but regal gait as Mavia made her way down
into the basin where the oasis flourished. When
they came to a stop, Khalif dismounted and
she hastily swept at the moisture in her eyes,
not wanting him to see how much being here
meant to her.

He reached for her and took her into his arms,
bringing her down from the horse, and stood
her barely an inch from him. He searched her
eyes in that way of his and she thought, *I want
you to look at me like that for ever.* Finally, she
looked away, hiding from his scrutiny, pretending to find the lake fascinating, when all she
could think of was him.

'Do you know where you are?' he asked, his
voice low but strong.

'This is where Hātem brought Catherine.' *Before she had to leave*, Star concluded silently,

trying to surf the wave of sadness that swept over her at the thought that she might soon be leaving too. 'Why did you bring me here?'

He looked over her shoulder, the desert swallowing the sigh that escaped his lips. It was as if he needed a moment to gather himself because when he turned back to her, his eyes were fierce. His hand cupped her cheek, holding her gaze—as if she could or would ever look away from him.

'I brought you here to remind you of the family who want you. Not just your sisters and your mother. But the family who knew you would come, following in their footsteps. To remind you of the one who trusted in her people, in the women of her blood and the women bound to those she loved. It is they who have kept her secret safe, ready and waiting for you. Not for anyone else. But you.

'You have been waited upon for over one hundred and fifty years, Star Soames. That is no small thing.'

She felt his words in her soul, as if something ancient had been woken beneath the desert and was reaching for her. So when Khalif delved into the bag on his saddle and retrieved a small velvet pouch her heart didn't pulse with surprise, it vibrated with an overwhelming feel of *rightness*. As if something predestined was finally coming to conclusion.

He took a necklace so familiar to Star from the pouch and held it up for her to inspect. She pressed slightly shaking fingers against her lips. This was what they had been looking for. It was the key to so much. To the past, to her mother's future… So much rested on such a small, beautiful thing. Khalif had been right. There were subtle differences, but it could have easily been mistaken for the one that she was wearing around her neck.

'May I?'

'Of course. It is now yours,' he said with a solemnity that felt ceremonial.

Taking it from him, she made her way blindly to the silks and woven rugs. She folded her legs beneath her, and she looped the gold chain over her head and brought the two pendants together.

She knew that they should fit together— Catherine's coded message had said as much— but she didn't quite… She ran her finger over the embossed pattern on the surface of the pendant and felt something shift. Pressing down released an indented piece of silver from the bottom of the pendant. She picked up Hātem's pendant and did the same. Staring at the two pendants, she didn't quite know what to do next. They needed to…

Khalif reached over. 'May I?' He seemed as lost in the task as she and she was happy to pass him the necklaces if it meant she could spend just a moment looking at the man who had given her more than he could ever know.

He turned the pendants in his hands, twisting and turning one piece while holding the other steady, and then, as if suddenly seeing how it could be, hooked one pendant into the other.

'Oh,' Star marvelled. Together the pieces created one key, the thick gold base forming the head and the two thinner silver offshoots forming the blade—the indentations becoming the ridges and notches that would fit into a lock.

Khalif pressed against the head of the key and the silver blade retracted into the body of the pendant. 'There. You can now wear them together.'

She stared at him, shaking her head in wonder. 'You don't like it?' he asked as if confused.

'I *do*! I love it. I just… I don't think I ever imagined actually finding it.'

I don't think I ever imagined actually finding you. *Finding the man I would love for the rest of my life.*

'Are you trying to tell me that you didn't believe your search would have a happy ending? And you call yourself a romantic,' he tsked.

She tried to swallow around the lump in her throat and a smile wobbled on her lips. 'Of course I do.'

He held up the necklace. 'Would you like me to—'

'Actually…' she said, rising quickly. 'I'd like to explore,' she exclaimed brightly, sure that the overly bright response had given her away, but he kindly let her go.

She couldn't take the necklace. Not yet. Because that would be the end of her search in Duratra. She would be done and wearing the necklace, holding it complete as the key would be the end of her time here. Especially as she was almost sure that she wasn't pregnant.

Khalif went to see Mavia, made sure that she had extra treats for carrying them both here. It hadn't been a long journey and she would have all the rest she needed, as he and Star would be driving out of here tomorrow.

He could see that Star had been affected by the necklace. He had been too, not imagining for a moment how it would feel to give away something that had been worn by the women of his family for over one hundred and fifty years. In doing so, it felt as if he'd entrusted part of his family to her.

Something red flashed in his eyeline and he knew that Star had undone the long thick plait of her hair. He clenched his jaw against the need to turn and look. Instead he worked on building a fire, ignoring the way ripples of water lapped against the fertile green border of the pool.

While his imagination painted images of mermaids with flowing red tresses and mystical creatures, he unpacked the food he had brought, placing it in the cool fridges running from the almost silent generator behind the tent.

The staff from Alhafa had worked through the night to make this happen, happy to do a kindness to the woman who had brought life back to the palace. He marvelled at how quickly, readily and easily she had become their Queen. But would it make her happy? Would being royal, being a princess in a foreign land, be right for her? Becoming a spectacle for the world to investigate, judge and find wanting, no matter how perfect she was. Her life would be on display and at risk and he knew that he could not do that to someone as pure and beautiful as her.

The fire took, the crackle and burn mixing with the chirps of the cicadas and the cry of the birds that stopped at the oasis on their journey across the desert. Wind gently rustled the leaves in the trees and water rippled and in his mind's eye he could see Star in the lake, her hair splayed on the surface and her body hidden from his gaze by the distortion of the liquid, no matter how pure.

His pulse pounded in his ears, blocking out the sounds of the desert. He cursed the wood beneath his hands because it wasn't smooth, freckled skin, soft as satin. A swift inhale followed a pinprick and he looked down to find a splinter in his thumb. Frowning, he removed the sliver of wood, watching the tiny bloom of blood before pressing it to his lips.

He'd never wanted a woman like this.

And he never would again.

'What happens if I'm not pregnant?'

Her voice, a little shaky, a lot tentative, came from behind him.

'You've only told me about what happens if I am.'

Because he'd not wanted to let her go.

He cleared his throat from his emotions' tight hold. 'You will return to Norfolk. I will return to the throne.'

'And that's it?'

'That's it.'

'I'll never see you again?'

She had posed it as a question that he chose instead to take as a statement, unable to bring himself to answer. Silently he roared his fury. Everything in him wanted to reach for her, just one last time. Not damning the consequences, but fully understanding them and facing them. His mind taunted that it was a gift, this one night, more than either he or she should have ever expected, but his heart berated him.

Maybe unconsciously he'd known that coming here wasn't just for her, but for him—to have this, to have *her*. He was selfish and she deserved so much more.

'Thank you for bringing me here.' The finality of her tone ate at him. It was as if she were saying goodbye.

'It was the least I could do.' He paused, knowing that his next words would open up a path neither should take, but both seemed powerless to resist. 'It may be the *only* thing I can do.'

'I understand,' she said quietly.

He spun around and pierced her with his gaze. 'Do you?' he demanded, furious with her, with himself. There wasn't anything about this that he understood.

'I do.'

It was then he took her in. Long red tresses soaked into ropes, lying flat against her skin. The long-sleeved white top almost transparent, revealing more than it concealed, pressed against her body the way he wanted to be.

His hands itched to reach for her, to take her, to pull her to him.

He was shaking his head as she took a step

forward and stopped, but he caught the way she masked her hurt in an instant and he cursed. She turned to walk away, but he was up and reaching for her before she could take a second step, turning her in his arms before she could take another breath, and punishing her with a kiss—punishing them both—before he could think again. She gasped into his mouth and he took it within him, locked it away because that was how she made him feel. Shocked, awed, thrilled... He wanted her to remember this moment for the rest of her life, because he already knew he would.

Her arms came up to his shirt, her hands fisted the cotton, pulling him to her, their passion frantic, needy and desperate.

His hands flew over her wet T-shirt, lifting and pulling to reach her skin, as if only that would soothe the burning need within him. Hand flat against the base of her spine, he pressed her into him, her taut nipples pebbling into his chest, her neck beneath his tongue and teeth, all the while her nails scratched trails of fire into his skin.

This was madness, utter madness, but neither seemed able or willing to stop.

He pulled back, long enough to let her lust filled gaze clear, having never seen anything more beautiful in his entire life. 'Star,' he warned as he took her in, pupils wide with desire, breath heaving. She looked utterly gorgeous.

Her name felt like an apology on his lips and she wanted to shout at him, yell and scream that she didn't want apologies, she wanted *this*. She wanted him. Needed him almost as much as her next breath. Before he could say another word, she pulled him to her, kissed him with all the passion she was capable of. All the surety she felt that, no matter the reality, no matter what happened tomorrow, he was the man she was supposed to love for the rest of her life.

His hands came around her waist, pressing against her hip and ass, and she lifted herself into them, wrapping her legs around his waist, glorying when she felt his erection at her core.

'Please,' she begged against his lips. 'Please, just tonight. Just this.'

He raised a hand to sweep her hair from her

face, holding her there, looking into her heart and soul. 'Of course.'

That night, Star was lost in a sea of pleasure. Fingers tangled, tongues danced, her skin was alive beneath his touch. She felt a fire building deep within her, expanding and filling her until the point where she couldn't contain it any more and an explosion of the most intangible beauty scattered her being across the star-covered desert.

Again and again he broke her into pieces, only to put her back together as something new, something different, and in that moment she knew she would never be the same again.

By the time the sun's rays cut a path through the tent's awning to rest against her skin, Star was aware that Khalif was no longer there. She dressed, her clothes feeling as if they didn't quite fit, and a sense that the morning—and the day—wouldn't quite be right fell against her soul.

She found him looking out across the desert.

'What are you…?' Her voice broke a little, her throat raw from screaming her pleasure through the night-time hours.

'I was making a wish. I—'

'Don't tell me,' she rushed out. 'It won't come true,' she warned.

'I was wishing not to be a prince.'

She swallowed the emotions begging to be released. It was a wish they knew couldn't and shouldn't come true.

'You are a wonderful prince. Conscientious, careful about others and what they think, thoughtful about doing the best thing possible for the greatest number of people. You will make a good ruler. Fair, strong, determined.'

Still looking out into the desert, he quirked his lip into a wry smile. 'Why do I hear a "but"?'

Star hurt for him, shook her head, but determined to say this to him. *For* him. 'You are not being *you*. You are being the Prince you think they want.'

'I am not my own any more. I am theirs,' he said, as if trying to explain himself to someone who refused to see his truth. When in reality he was simply refusing to see hers.

'You could be the ruler you want to be, if you are willing to stand by the consequences.'

She knew how that sounded, but Star really wasn't thinking of herself. She was thinking of the man who had already begun to lose himself under the weight of the crown. 'I wish I could have seen you before.'

'What,' he scoffed, 'as the disreputable play-boy?'

'No. Just the boy.'

Khalif reared back as if she had struck him. He was about to reply when the roar of a Jeep's engine cut through the desert.

They were out of time.

CHAPTER TEN

'SO, STAR'S APPOINTMENT with Maya is tomorrow?' Amin asked for the hundredth time that day. Even Khalif's other members of staff glared at the bespectacled man.

Reza leaned against the wall of the meeting room, refusing to take his eyes from Khalif, who was spending an unnecessary amount of time trying to ignore that fact.

'And you know she can't attend the event tonight?'

Khalif was going to have to see a dentist before the week was out. And Amin might be paying a visit to the doctor. He opened his mouth to speak when he felt Reza's hand on his shoulder, as if holding him back from the violence he wanted to inflict.

'I think we all understand that. In the meantime, let's take a short break before reconvening for the run-through for tonight's event.'

The quiet authority of Reza's tone had the

desired effect on his staff and the opposite effect on Khalif.

'I don't need you to speak for me,' he growled.

'Of course you don't. But you also don't need a mutiny on your hands, which is what will happen if you push your staff any harder.'

'It is no harder than I push myself.'

'You're right. It is considerably less. But that doesn't mean either is manageable.' His best friend let go of the hold on his shoulder as the last staff member left the room. 'What are you more afraid of? That she is pregnant or she isn't?'

'Does it matter? I couldn't do this to her,' he said, finally saying it out loud. 'I know what it is like to have that freedom taken away and I can't...' Khalif shook his head.

'I know the sacrifices you have—'

'Sacrifices? I changed *everything*! I *stopped* everything.' Khalif stared at his best friend in disbelief. Finally, after three years, it poured forth. 'I gave up an international business I had built from scratch, I dropped everything and came home. I buried my brother and Samira in front of the world's press. I made phone calls and shook hands within hours of their funeral… I did what I had to and would do it again. But Reza, I couldn't *breathe*, let alone grieve in the way I wanted.' And for *who* I wanted, he finally admitted to himself. 'This? It's like being in a straitjacket, folded in on yourself, cramped, confined. The expectation of everyone, the watching, the pressure. How on earth can you think I would willingly put that on someone as innocent as Star?'

Reza stared at him with deep understanding and sympathy. He placed his hand on Khalif's shoulder, the weight both comforting and steadying. He nodded once and Khalif knew that his best friend understood.

'Okay,' Reza said simply. 'Then let's talk about how this holographic presentation is going to work, because that is going to blow their minds.'

It felt strange to be back in Khalif's suite. Especially since everything that had happened between then and now had begun to feel like a dream. She was on the balcony, the late afternoon sun sinking into her skin, warming her pleasantly…but not quite enough.

She rolled her shoulders, bracing her hands against the balustrade, eyes searching the horizon. The view of the city looked a little different now that she knew out there, beyond the stretches of golden sand, the sloping dunes and hazy blue skies, was a desert palace seen only by a few and an oasis that would always be in her heart.

She glanced at the rucksack containing everything she had brought with her and one new item. She had returned the connected pendants to the velvet bag and was yet to be able to wear them, putting off the moment until she truly knew that she would be going home. The necklace now had a double chain, as if it would always acknowledge that it had needed two people to come together to make it whole.

She felt a tide of anxiety washing against her soul, back and forth like the sea. She was nervous for Khalif, knowing how much the reveal of his plans for the memorial meant to him. So much so that she'd borne the look of guilt he'd worn as he'd explained why she couldn't come to the event that night with understanding and acceptance. Both of which she truly felt. But it had hurt nonetheless.

Yet it hurt in a different way to how she had felt alone in the palace in the desert. This was not the sense of shame and rejection she had felt because of her grandparents, it was more a sense of inevitable ache. A sense of loss that was down to fate rather than intention. Where once Catherine had been forced to do her duty, now it was Khalif's turn—and Star honestly couldn't have argued against either.

He'd offered her a way that she could still see the presentation, which she would take, because it was his moment and she wouldn't take that away from him. Which was why there, on the balcony, facing the desert, she sent a prayer to Catherine and Hātem, and Faizan and Samira, to look out for him that night.

There was a knock on the door. Star had been expecting it, but it still made her jump. She turned back into the room to find Maya closing the door behind her. She smiled at Star, who braced herself.

'I was hoping you could help me with something. Do you think it's possible to take the test today and for it still to be accurate?'

Khalif flexed his jaw, hoping to relieve the ache in his cheeks from the perfunctory smiles he'd masked himself in.

Samira's father, Abbad, had been casting grim glances his way since the first guests had arrived and his wife's vacant gaze wasn't any better. The only time he'd felt himself relax was when Nadya had winked at him and run off to play hide-and-seek amongst the legs of the guests. His parents were thankfully preoccupied by small talk with dignitaries and international diplomats.

'It is a stunning design,' Reza said quietly, having stuck by his side the entire afternoon.

'I know.'

'You should be proud.'

'And she should be *here*,' he growled, his tone grating his throat.

'There are three hundred people present, the Duratrian press both inside and outside the palace, along with more than a few representatives of the international newspapers. You think that a woman with hair like the sun would go unnoticed in here?' Reza reminded him. 'Tonight is about Faizan, Samira…and you. *After* tonight,' he pressed, 'is another matter entirely.'

You are wrong, my friend, Khalif thought, no matter how much he wished it weren't the case.

Khalif stepped up to the podium and the audience grew quiet and turned to face him. He looked out across the faces he could see beneath the bright powerful glare of lighting trained on the stage. He felt the hairs on the back of his neck lift, his heartbeat stumbled and while he didn't know how, or where, Khalif knew that Star was here. He took a breath.

'Ladies and gentlemen. My family and I are honoured that you could be here tonight. For some, it may have seemed like a long time coming,' he acknowledged to the gentle murmur rippling across the guests. 'However, I truly believe that my brother and Samira deserved such consideration. The…hole they left in the lives of their family and friends is immeasurable and it was important to respect that grief. Faizan and Samira touched so many lives. They didn't just merge two families, but they brought two countries together and two beautiful princesses into this world.

'Growing up with Faizan was no mean feat,' he said, to the slight laughter of the crowd. 'He was focused, driven, bright, intelligent, compassionate. And I can see those qualities already in Nadya and Nayla. Faizan always knew what legacy he wanted to leave behind him. One of peace in the present and hope for the future. Hope not just for his people, but his planet. And Samira? She was always smiling, always ready to be the balance in disagreements, always ready to bridge the gap between her husband the Prince and the man who loved his family and his people above all else. Samira and Faizan were proud, loving and very conscious of their countries.

'She was the bridge and he the river that ran deep beneath it and that is how I, and I hope all of you, will remember them.'

He stepped back from the stage and allowed the lights to dim. The gentle hum of excitement building from the crowd momentarily stopped in awe when they saw the first images from the holographic display.

Khalif heard the words of his pre-recorded voice-over explain about the area between Duratra and Udra that had long since been aban-

doned. It was a kind of no man's land where the
river, coming from the Red Sea, cut between
Duratra and Samira's home country.

The hologram showed images of what the
country looked like now and slowly how the
area would be cleared, cleaned and prepared
for what was to come. Over the next few minutes, the graphics showed a bridge being built
over the river between the two neighbouring
countries. Beautiful plants and lush greenery
developed along both sides of the banks as well
as each side of the wide bridge. Oohs and aahs
came from the audience as they could see the
trees grow, healthy and strong and high on top
of the bridge.

'There will be no cars or vehicles in the area.
It will be completely pedestrianised. Wildlife
will be introduced—birds, insects and eventu-
ally larger animals—all cared for by specially
trained staff who will provide guided free tours
for any visitor.

'It will be a sanctuary. A place for people to
come and honour the memory of Faizan and
Samira, and the investment in the future that
was always so very important to them. It is
the paradise they would have wanted for their

children, and it is what their children wanted to honour and remember their parents.'

His family needed this, his country needed—*deserved*—stability, unity, cohesion and healing and he knew deep down in his bones that this would be the first step.

Khalif looked out into the audience, touched by the overwhelming emotion he felt rising up to meet his own. Goosebumps pebbled his skin and he thought that he saw a flash of red, looking up in time to see the movement of a curtain at the balcony near the private suites on the upper level.

'Uncle Kal… Uncle Kal!'

He turned just in time to catch Nadya, who had thrown herself at him in wild abandon.

'You had the birds!' Nadya's voice was a little muffled from where her face was pressed against his stomach and she gripped his waist like a limpet. Nayla, the shyer of the two, stood with a massive grin and wide eyes showing her delight, standing with one foot tucked behind the other.

'And flowers,' he said to her, and she nodded enthusiastically.

'Will it be bright blue and pink like the hologriff?'

Kal didn't have the heart to correct her. 'Well, maybe we can speak to the designers about that. We have quite a bit to do before we get to that point.'

Over his nieces' heads, he saw his parents making their way towards him. Unease stirred briefly but then he grounded himself. He knew that he had done the right thing—not because it pleased everyone, but because he felt it in his gut. The memorial would be doing the right thing by his nieces and by Faizan and Samira.

'My son,' his mother, Hafsa, greeted him, her eyes crinkling the fine lines at the corners into fans. He wasn't sure whether it was a consequence of losing his brother, or valuing the family he did have and the love he felt for them, but his heart felt torn—between being here with his family and being with the woman upstairs. And he knew that neither deserved half a heart.

It took him an hour to extricate himself from the gala, but he couldn't have said that he'd tried too hard. He had felt it. Something in the air had shifted. A kind of knowledge, or awareness, had begun to creep over him, without him knowing specifically what it was. He just knew that he had to get to Star.

His heart was pounding as he made his way through the private areas of the palace, but his footsteps were slow and purposeful. Something inside him was roaring to get out, but he hardly made a sound. He smiled at the staff and few family members he passed, though in his mind's eye he saw only one thing…one person.

He closed the door to his suite behind him and stopped. He inhaled the scent of her on the air, wondering if that might be the last time he did so. He didn't have to look, to know that she was out on the balcony. She loved that view almost as much as he did.

He took two steps into the room and paused. Letting himself see her. The way her hair twisted in the gentle desert breeze. From this angle she stood at the balcony amongst the stars and he bit his lip to stop himself from saying something, not wanting to spoil the moment—for her or him.

She turned slightly to the side, as if sensing his presence, and wiped at something on her cheek that he didn't quite see, so caught up in the sight of her.

'What are you doing here?' she asked.

'I live here,' he said, but the joke fell flat. 'I was worried.'

'About the presentation?'

'No, that went well. Really well.' He closed the distance between them as she turned to face him fully. 'Everyone loved it.'

'Of course they did.' She smiled and his heart ached at the easy acceptance and surety ringing in her voice. 'You should probably get back,' she insisted, 'it's still early.'

'I was wrong,' he said, offering her all that he could. 'To ask you to stay here.'

'You weren't and you know it,' she replied without malice or anger. This was Star as he'd never seen her before. Regal, poised and absolutely breathtaking. And that was when he saw the necklace, the double strands of the chain on either side of the pendant making it something strangely beautiful. And instinctively he braced himself against something he felt he already knew.

Star searched his features, her eyes running over his head, shoulders, down the length of his body, consuming as much of him as she possibly could. There was no way Kal could have let her be there at the event that evening. She understood a little of that duty now. How the crowd had looked up to him, watched him, hung on every word. How they had cried and sighed their appreciation of his plans for the memorial. He had given them a focal point for their grief and the beginning of the healing process. She supposed in some way she was about to give herself the same.

'I'm—' Khalif started.

'I'm not pregnant,' she interrupted before he could say anything more.

He simply held her gaze as if he had felt it in the same way she had. When Maya had presented her with the results of the test, Star hadn't been surprised by the fact she wasn't carrying Khalif's baby, but by the extent to which she'd actually been wanting to. Not once had she let herself hope or believe because… because, she realised now, she had never wanted anything more in her life.

'Maya assured me the test was accurate.'

He closed the space between them in just two steps, drawing so close to her, only inches really. It was as if he wanted to touch her, reach

for her, just as much as she wanted him to...
but couldn't. Wouldn't.

In one breath, Star was lost just to the sense
of him. His exhale shuddered against her cheek,
before he turned to stand beside her, facing
the desert. She placed her hands on the stone
balcony close to his, their little fingers almost
touching, but her heart knew the distance might
as well have been a chasm.

Go...go now.

But she couldn't. She forced herself to stay,
refusing to turn and run. She was a reader. She
was a romantic. And, whether it was foolish
or not, she had hope. All the things they'd experienced—an impossible meeting, ancestors
torn apart by duty, families brought back together by fate. She had found Catherine's Duratra out there in the desert. Khalif had found
her necklace...

'So that's it then.' His voice was rough and
dark in the dusk.

She felt as if she'd conjured up the words
herself. The first steps of the dance that would
see them either spending the rest of their lives
together or...

'Is it?'

'Star…' he warned.

'No, Khalif. It's a question I am asking you. *Is* that it then?'

She refused to look at him, even though he was staring at her hard, trying to get her to face him. But she wouldn't. Couldn't. Because he'd see. He'd see all that she wasn't quite ready for him to see.

'It's funny how people behave when they think they don't have a choice,' she said to the desert. 'It traps them, makes them feel helpless, makes them behave in ways that aren't authentic to them. Ways that aren't right for them.'

'You can't consider my life to have choices.'

'Why not?' she demanded. 'Look what you did when you realised that you had a choice for Faizan and Samira's memorial? Look at the incredibly beautiful, amazing thing you have set in motion. Do you not think that we could—'

'It's not the same. *Everyone* in my family, every heir to the throne has been in the same position,' he growled.

'The definition of madness is doing the same thing over and over again and expecting different results.'

'Why do you think I'm expecting different results?' He looked at her, genuinely confused. 'There were no disastrous results for my parents. And Faizan and Samira's marriage was a very happy, fruitful one.'

'But not for you. Not the hurt it caused you,' she half cried. 'Would you force this on your nieces? Would you expect them to marry for duty rather than love?'

'No! I'm doing this so that they can have that option for themselves.'

'Really? You're not doing this because it's easier than being true to yourself?'

His gaze met hers in a fiery clash, the golden flecks in his umber eyes swirling like a sandstorm. 'Star—'

But she couldn't listen to him. She had to press on. This was her last chance. Her only chance. 'Because I suppose you can't really fail if you're always trying to please everyone else. If you're being everything other people need, then it's their need that's failed, not you. And you'll never know.'

'Know what?'

'You'll never know how incredible you could be if you were just yourself.'

* * *

Her voice rang with such sincerity, such hope and such optimism he half wanted to believe it himself. It was seductive, what she was saying. Be himself, choose her, be a great ruler. But she was wrong.

'I was myself,' he bit out angrily. 'For three years, I wined and womanised my way around Europe. Is that the kind of ruler Duratra deserves? Is that the kind of man you want?' His voice had become a shout.

'You were hurt. Your entire family condoned a marriage between your brother and your first love. Of course you acted out,' she said, desperately grasping for justifications for his terrible behaviour.

'Acted out? Is that what…?' He ground his teeth together, hating the way that her words ran through his head and heart. Her understanding, her belief in him crucified him, made a mockery of every single choice he'd made since, tearing him in half between what he so desperately wanted and what he felt he needed to do.

And he was furious. In that moment, he wanted to bring down the palace, smash and burn everything—anything to make the questions stop. So he did the only thing he could do.

'I know you think being a prince means that—'

'Don't,' she said, the single word a plea. 'Don't use that—'

'I know you think being a prince means that magical adventures await and love comes with singing birds and talking clocks,' he said, looking away from the tears brimming in her eyes. 'But it's not. It's *not*, Star,' he insisted. 'It's constantly putting the country first. It is making a marriage that is strategic and for the good of this country.'

'And there is nothing strategic about marrying me?'

'No.' He shook his head. 'There just isn't.'

'Your happiness is not strategic? It doesn't count?'

'No. It never has,' he said with the same sense of acceptance that had descended the moment he'd realised he was to take the throne.

'If you allow that feeling, that anger and resentment about Samira marrying Faizan to shape everything you do, the choices you make—'

'Don't say her...' He couldn't finish the sentence so instead he bit off his words, his tongue. It had been cruel, and he knew it. The hurt on Star's features was two red slashes on her cheeks.

'You can attack my dreams but I can't challenge your fears? Is it yourself that you're punishing by refusing to listen to your heart, or someone else? Why would you damn yourself to unhappiness?'

Why wouldn't she stop? Why was she pushing him like this?

'Is it because,' she pressed on, 'if you can have a happy marriage, if *you* can choose who you marry, then so could Faizan? Then it would mean that your wonderful, incredible brother made the wrong choice and it hurt you?'

'Wow, you're really going for it tonight, aren't you?' he scoffed bitterly, wondering what else she was going to drag him through. Because being angry with her was easier than feeling the truth of her words.

'Of course I am. My heart is on the line. My love for you. Can't you see that?'

White-hot pain slashed across his chest, a death blow that wouldn't end his life but could still stop his heart. Because only in the moments when his heart wasn't beating could he find the strength to be cruel enough to force her to go.

'Love? In two weeks?' he taunted. 'That really *is* a romance,' he said, forcing scepticism into his tone that burned all the way down. 'Then again, it's easier to fall in love when the fantasy can never live up to the reality, isn't it? You hide in your romances, preferring them to reality. But I don't have that luxury, Star.'

She looked as if she'd been struck and the only decent thing he could do was bear witness to it. He hated himself more than he ever had done before, but her words had taken hold and weren't letting go. He couldn't follow them, not now, not yet, and he greatly feared what would happen when he did. He felt like a bull, head down and ploughing forward, because anything else meant that he had to confront his feelings, her feelings.

Confront *her.* The way she was always challenging him, demanding of him, expecting him to be better when he couldn't.

'You're right. I do have choices. And I'm sorry that the one I need to make causes you pain.' His words were mechanical, forced. She knew it, he knew it, but there was also, inevitably, a truth beneath them. 'But I would make this choice every time. I choose Duratra.'

She wiped at a large, fat tear that escaped down her cheek, the action reminding him of what he'd seen when he'd first come onto the balcony. And he realised in that moment that she'd been crying before they'd talked. Before he'd said the horrible things, because she'd always known how the conversation would play out. She had known, before she'd even told him that she wasn't pregnant, what his reaction would be.

As she walked from the balcony, out of the suite and the palace, he realised then that he'd got it so terribly wrong. She was not a coward, hiding in romance. She was strong enough and brave enough to face reality. Stronger and braver than him.

The blow to his stomach and heart was doubly hard, physical and emotional, and he collapsed to the floor, his back against the cold, unyielding stone balcony that both held him up and anchored him while everything in him wanted to run after her.

CHAPTER ELEVEN

AT AROUND TWO in the morning Khalif found himself in one of the larger family suites, looking for whisky. He'd not had it in his quarters for three years. He'd not even had a drink in three years. But tonight he needed one.

He opened the door to the alcohol cabinet his father kept for visitors, retrieved the weighty cut glass tumbler and poured himself a satisfyingly large couple of inches of whisky. He swirled it around the glass as he sat, letting the peaty alcoholic scent waft up to meet him, his taste buds exploding with expectation and his conscience delaying the moment of gratification as punishment.

What had he done?

He was about to take a sip when the door to the living room opened and he looked up to find his father surveying him with something like pity.

'I haven't seen you drink since before Faizan died.'

It was on the tip of his tongue to lash out and say he'd not actually had the drink yet, but that felt churlish. Instead, he watched his father go to the cabinet and retrieve the whisky bottle and pour himself an equally large glass. 'I haven't seen you drink since…'

'Faizan's funeral?' his mother asked as she too came into the room. Both men's faces held the same look, as if they'd just been caught with their hands in a cookie jar. Never had they more appeared like father and son. 'Oh, don't be silly. If I was outraged at this, I'd have never survived the first six months as your Queen,' she teased the men in her life, leaning to press a kiss to her husband's cheek.

Bakir grinned conspiratorially at his son and took a seat in the large leather chair opposite Khalif as his wife perched on the arm.

Then the light dimmed from his eyes and Bakir took a breath. 'Faizan and Samira,' he said, raising his glass.

Khalif raised his and blinked back the sudden wetness in his eyes, swallowing his grief with the first powerful mouthful of whisky.

'Khalif, we are—'

He held his hand up to ward off his father's words but, though he paused, Bakir pressed on.

'We are so very proud of you. The memorial is...'

'Perfect,' his mother concluded, her smile watery and her eyes bright with unshed tears. She sniffed and her husband handed her a handkerchief without breaking eye contact with his son. 'Where on earth did you get the idea?' she asked.

Khalif clenched his jaw before prising the words from his conscience. 'A friend. She asked about Faizan and Samira, encouraged me to remember them. She suggested I talk to Nadya and Nayla about what they might like to have in the memorial.'

'She sounds very clever,' his mother observed.

'She is,' Khalif agreed.

'Did she encourage you to do anything else?' his father asked.

Through gritted teeth, he said, 'To be myself. To stop trying to be you or Faizan,' he confessed.

'She really *is* a wise woman,' his mother said,

the smile in her voice evident. His father scoffed and Khalif's head jerked up to stare at his parents. He wanted to yell at them, to say that it wasn't a laughing matter.

'That's only because you said a very similar thing to me many years ago,' Bakir groused.

'*And* you barely listened to me,' his mother complained.

Khalif's head was swimming and it wasn't from the alcohol. 'What are you talking about? I thought you had an arranged marriage?'

Bakir cast a level gaze at his son. 'Well, a lot of work went into making it look that way, so I'm glad it was successful.'

Khalif couldn't work out whether his father was being sarcastic or ironic.

'We had met before,' his mother explained on a slightly flustered, and somewhat guilty, exhale. 'Before the engagement.'

'Your mother told me that if I couldn't orchestrate a good enough reason for us to get married, how would I ever manage to run a country? So I found a way.' Bakir shrugged. 'She challenged me then, and has each day since.'

His father stared at him intently and sighed

deeply, as if not looking forward to what he was about to say. 'We all knew that you cared for Samira and she for you.'

'Cared?' Khalif almost choked, anger gripping him almost instantly.

'But we also knew that she wasn't right for you,' his father continued. 'Us, Faizan and even Samira.'

Khalif fisted the glass and clamped his jaw shut. He was furious. Not with his father but because he knew that his father was right.

'You were the younger son, Khalif. The one protected from the lessons and the rigours of royal instruction. In hindsight, that was a mistake. I...' Bakir seemed to struggle for words for the first time Khalif could remember. Finding his strength, he pressed on. 'My father taught me nothing about ruling a country, for fear that I would try to usurp him. My learning curve was steep. I didn't want... Faizan to have the same difficulties. I never thought—'

Hafsa placed her hand on her husband's and their fingers intertwined.

Khalif put the glass down on the side table, reached forward and placed his hand over theirs, joining them in their grief but also their love. He was ready to hear whatever his father had to say.

'I knew how much you wanted to be part of Faizan's lessons, but I feared the distraction. So you were given every freedom in compensation. And while you didn't want those freedoms, wouldn't have chosen them for yourself, you *did* have them. You were spoilt by that freedom—wholly unintentionally.

'No one challenged you, not even Samira. You had a special bond, no one can deny that, and we all loved her greatly. But she would have let you do anything, and you would have run roughshod over her all the while, never needing to do more, to be more, or better. You wouldn't have been good for each other.'

Khalif had braced for it and his father's words still hurt. But he couldn't deny the truth in them. All this time he had taunted Star for romanticism, but had he not done the same? Had he not fantasised the perfect, but mainly imagined, future with Samira? Had that not been the truest form of romanticism? All the while Star had questioned him, teased him about his preconceptions, challenged him to make better decisions, to follow his gut, encouraged him to make mistakes and learn from fixing them. And with that thought hope bloomed and his heart soared.

'What is that look on your face?'

'I've made a terrible mistake, Father.'

'Then why do you look so happy?'

'Because now I get to fix it,' he said, the smile lifting his lips and his heart soaring for the first time that evening.

'And how are you planning to do that?'

'Romance books. I need romance books.'

'I think he's gone mad,' his father said to his wife, looking deeply concerned. But his mother's eyes were lit with sparkles that only reminded Khalif of Star.

Star plucked at a loose thread on the long end of the pashmina she wore, her eyes sore and finally dry. She had sandwiched the phone between her ear and shoulder to leave both hands free so she could tackle the frayed cotton.

'I can be on a plane in two hours.'

'Mum, you don't drive, your bank account is pretty much empty, you hate carbon emissions more than you hate the Tories, and my plane leaves in three hours, so I'll be back in England before you would even get here.'

'Your sister said exactly the same thing,' Mariam Soames grumbled.

'It's the thought that counts, Mum. Star sounded happy?'

'Yes, she did. I'm looking forward to meeting this Chalendar. And I'm looking forward to having all my girls back in the same country and under the same roof. I don't like the idea of Summer at that house all on her own.'

Star marvelled that her mother had grown up in the sprawling, dilapidated Norfolk estate and insisted on calling it a 'house', despite the fact it had over thirty bedrooms. Star's fingers left the cotton thread and lifted to the gold ropes of the chain at her neck.

How she and her sisters had thought they would have been able to keep the search for the missing jewels from their mother a secret, she had no idea. It had hurt to reveal Elias's manipulations to their mother, but when Skye had called them from France they'd known that it was time to tell Mariam everything. She had been as angry as much as Mariam Soames was capable of being angry with her daughters, which was about as long as it took to sigh.

'I know what you girls are trying to do—'

'We're so nearly there, Mum,' Star whispered, more of a plea than a promise. 'Skye has the map of the secret passageways, I have the key—we just need to find them now.'

'I know, Star. I just…' There was a pause on the end of the line and Star imagined her mother shifting her shawl around her shoulders. 'I've decided that I'm going to move in with Samantha for a bit.'

'Really? I thought you might want to—'

'Live with my just-beginning-to-find-their-feet, lovely and well-meaning daughters?' Mariam replied and Star couldn't help but smile at the laugh in her mother's voice.

The words *just beginning to find their feet* really struck Star. It was a little too close to what she'd hoped to achieve by coming to Duratra—to prove that she could stand on her own two feet—and Star felt as if she both had and hadn't.

'Samantha has known me for years. She's perfectly capable of putting up with me for a little longer,' Mariam said assuredly but without thought. A sob rose suddenly and shockingly in Star's chest. 'I didn't mean it like that,' her mother said.

'I know,' Star promised.

'We are going to beat this.'

'*I* know,' Star replied, forcing a smile to her lips in the hope that it would be heard in her voice. 'Actually... I was thinking about moving out of the flat and setting up somewhere on my own. Do you think that Skye would be okay with that? I mean—' Star struggled to find the words to explain her sudden need to hold onto that bit of independence she'd discovered in Duratra '—with Summer away at uni most of the year...'

Her mother sighed. 'I think that Skye will worry but, with her engagement, it's more than likely that she'll be relocating to France. If it feels right for you, my love, then we will all support you one hundred per cent.'

'I think it might scare me a little, but it's something I would like very much. I love Skye and Summer but...they need to see that I am capable of being independent.' Star sighed, all the pent-up emotion pouring from her chest in one breath. 'Mum...' she started, nervous as to the answer. 'Do you think Kal was right? Have I been hiding?'

'No, my love,' said her mother, her voice warm and reassuring. 'You haven't hidden in romances. You've been learning. Learning what you like, what you want, and what you will and won't put up with.

'Romances don't warp our expectations, they raise them. And there is nothing wrong with that. They show us that it is okay to put ourselves, our desires, at the forefront of our intentions. They show us not to be ashamed of our wants. Whether that want is emotional, practical or sexual, my love.' While cringing at her mother using words like sexual, because that was *never* going to be okay, Star knew what she meant. 'You should never have been made to feel ashamed or rejected. Not by your grandparents, nor your prince.'

'He's not my prince, Mum.'

'They should be the ones who feel shame, Star,' Mariam carried on as if Star hadn't interrupted. 'You reached out to make a connection with honesty, integrity, love and hope. They are lesser for turning you away. You are worthy of someone who reaches for you.'

Star smiled at the old family joke and she couldn't help the flood of memories overwhelming her. Khalif reaching to take her from his horse...the incredible gift of taking her to the desert, giving her a connection to Catherine that felt fated...making her feel loved and wanted by her ancestors, even if he hadn't been capable of it himself.

She allowed herself to feel that love, for her heart to swell with it as she promised to call her mother the moment she touched down in England. But as she ended the call, clutching the double-chained necklace which she kept interlocked together, she forced herself to face reality.

He had also left her alone without barely a thought and kept her hidden even when he knew he shouldn't. He had pushed her away with cruel words because it was easier than fighting his demons. And he had made her feel just as unwanted as wanted. But, despite the hurt and pain she felt, she knew he had been right.

He couldn't have chosen her any more than Catherine could have chosen Hātem, but she couldn't help but feel that there was a sense of wrongness about repeating the same decisions that had been made by their ancestors.

She glanced at the departures board, frowning when she noticed that there was a delay sign against her flight that hadn't been there two minutes ago. Everything in her wanted to go home, but she couldn't shake the feeling that her home was no longer in England.

Perhaps the desert sand had got into her blood somehow. She shook off the curious notion as she noticed a few heads turn towards the entrance of the airport. There was a rise and fall in murmurs, like the dip and swell of the sea and, while she tried to ignore it, more and more heads were turning and she began to hear audible gasps.

A group turned into a crowd and nearly forty people were now gathered near the entrance, all focusing on one point and then parting like the waves to make way for...for...

Oh, my...

The first thing she saw was Khalif, his eyes blazing with purpose and something she dared not name. Then she saw the horse. Mavia, she recognised, decked out in a saddle that had more gold and jewels on it than Star had thought possible. What on earth was he doing here on a horse?

The gold brocade *bisht* over his *thawb* was immaculate, and the *keffiyeh* around his head picked out the same gold tones, making him impossibly regal and almost too handsome for her to look at. Star focused on as many details as possible, trying to ignore the burst of hope that swelled in her heart.

Mavia lifted her head as if to say hello and Star soon found herself within metres of the incredible animal and her rider. The crowd who had at first held up their phones to capture a picture of their Prince, soon began to lower them one by one, some being nudged by a neighbour, others of their own volition, and Star could have sworn that she'd seen Amin somewhere in the midst of it.

Khalif swung ever so gracefully from Mavia and took two steps towards her before dropping to his knee, much to the gasped delight of the crowd.

'Kha—' Star clamped her mouth shut, took a moment and tried again. 'Your Highness,' she said—clearly unable to ignore the royal on bended knee right in front of her.

Once again, she felt the familiar search of his eyes across her face, her body, as if trying to take her in all at once and it not being enough. At least that was what she felt she was doing to him. Searching, hoping…waiting.

'Miss Soames,' Khalif said, loudly enough for the entire crowd to hear, 'I stepped down, trying not to look at you, as if you were a Star, yet I saw you, like a Star, without even looking.'

The words were poetic and lovely, but familiar and— She frowned. Wait, was that *Anna Karenina*? If not in full, then near enough. She opened her mouth to ask, but he pressed on.

'Because whatever our souls are made of, yours and mine are the same…' he insisted with a smile, as if confident she would recognise that as Brontë. 'Because I assure you, I was asleep, until I fell in love.'

Star couldn't stop the roll of her eyes. 'I refuse to believe that you read *War and Peace* in the last twenty-four hours, Khalif,' she chided.

'It might have been the crib notes version, but still… A very clever romance novel once said that "It is better to love wisely, no doubt: but to love foolishly is better than not to be able to love at all."'

'Thackeray,' she whispered, the goosebumps spreading from her toes to her shoulders.

'"In vain I have struggled. It will not do. My feelings will *not* be repressed. You must allow me to tell you how ardently I admire and love you."'

She couldn't smile—not yet. In spite of all the hope and all the love she felt in that moment, she needed more. *'Pride and Prejudice*? Really? Is that how you come to me? With the words of others on your tongue?' she demanded.

'No,' he replied, with no hurt or censure in his eyes, as if he'd expected her to challenge him. 'That was just to get your attention.'

'And you didn't think the horse would be enough?' she teased.

The crowds laughed a little, reminding her that they had an audience.

'Do you want to go somewhere a little more private?' she whispered to him.

'I am right where I need to be, Star Soames,' he said, his voice loud, confident and carrying, causing tears to gather in her eyes. 'And no. The horse was not enough,' Khalif said, as if all joking was done and now he wanted her to know the sincerity of his words. Of his love.

'I'm not completely sure that there will ever be enough ways for me to tell you how much I love you and why. But I'm going to try. You exploded into my life, dragging me by the arm and leading me to places I never expected.'

She blushed at the memory of how she had first encountered the Prince of Duratra, not having a single clue that he had been anything other than another tourist.

'You put your trust and faith in me from the first, though I had not earned such a gift. You experienced, in the harshest of ways, the constraints of royal life and bore them without question, without argument or censure. You taught me things I didn't know I still needed to learn and helped me to rediscover the things I knew but had forgotten. And in return I made you doubt your dreams. I will not forgive myself for that. I made you feel unwanted, and I promise never to let you feel that again. I made you feel shame by hiding you away, but *I* was the one who should have felt shame for my actions. So now I vow to you, before the people of my country, that I will spend every day for the rest of my life being worthy of you—even if you choose not to do me the honour of becoming my wife.'

Star looked down at him, bent at the knee on the floor of the airport, and still the most amazing thing she'd ever seen.

'What do you say?' he asked, and the flash of uncertainty nearly broke her heart.

'Well, I'm tempted to say that you should never ask someone to marry you in the negative, but that's only really because you asked me to challenge you.'

A gasp of consternation that sounded very much like Amin caused Khalif to smile. He smiled because it was exactly how he'd hoped Star would reply, loving that she still surprised him and kept him pushing for more, for better. Her smile was a little wobbly, but her eyes were bright, clear and full of love he felt to his very soul.

'Surely,' she said, her voice carrying without effort, 'my faith in my dreams would not have been that strong if it was shaken by one conversation? In as much as my sense of self would have to have been weak if I blamed you for making me feel unwanted or ashamed. And how could that be, when you were the one to show me that I have been looked for all my life, wanted and cared for by my family through centuries? When you were the one who has shown me that reality can be even more romantic and wonderful than fantasy?'

She shook her head as if in wonder that he hadn't, couldn't see what she saw in him, her love for him. He got to his feet and reached for her, cupping her jaw in his hands, taking what felt like his first breath since the early hours of that morning as she rested her head against his palm.

'Ask me again,' Star whispered, her eyes locked with his, lit with love and a happiness that made his chest burn.

'Will you, Star Soames, be my wife, my love, my partner, my Queen?'

'Yes,' she said as a tear of happiness rolled down her cheek.

'I love you so much,' he whispered so that only she could hear.

'Good,' she replied, with a cheeky smile that made his heart soar. 'Now, please, can you take me home?'

'To England?'

She shook her head and smiled, playing with the strands of the necklace. 'No. To Alhafa... to the desert.'

'As you wish,' he said, his heart full of love and peace.

'*After* we have couriered the necklace to my sisters,' Star said, with light sparkling in her eyes.

'I know just the man to do it... Amin?'

EPILOGUE

STAR STOOD ON the balcony of the suite she shared with her husband at Alhafa, gazing out at the view of the desert she would never tire of.

She could hear her husband in the shower, and the scent of eucalyptus oil was heavy on the steam escaping from the bathroom. She inhaled deeply, trying to catch it before it disappeared, loving the scent she always associated with her husband.

She blinked away the jet lag from the time difference between Duratra and the Dordogne, smiling as images from Skye's wedding to Benoit Chalendar filled her mind and heart. Her older sister had looked breathtakingly beautiful, the love she felt for her husband shining so bright it touched each and every guest. Their mother had cried through the entire ceremony, just as she had at Star's wedding, stopping only for a short while to laugh at Summer's daughter Catherine who, despite her mother's intentions, absolutely stole the show. But only for a heartbeat. And none of the sisters would have had it any differently.

The relief following her mother's successful treatment had been both shocking and surprising in its intensity. Khalif had been there and supported her through an aftershock that she had not expected, as all the fear, the hurt and pain she had kept at bay during their search for the jewels had run free only *after* they had accomplished all they had set out to do. Khalif had held her, comforted her, reassured her, soothed her and loved her through it all.

Star absentmindedly smoothed a hand over her stomach as she looked down at the sapphire wedding ring on her fourth finger of her other hand, remembering not only Khalif's proposal but her own magical wedding day six months before.

A smile lit her features and her heart as she thought of how the whole of Duratra had turned out to watch the wedding of Sheikh Khalif and his bride. Celebrations had filled the streets for days and Star had found a welcome and acceptance she could never have imagined. The love that Khalif had shown her in the year since they had first met was something wondrous to her and she thought she'd never have too much of it.

She smiled now as she remembered how protective he had been of her, especially in the first few months of their engagement and marriage. She would never forget the look of shock on Khalif's features as she'd requested Amin as her personal advisor. He had asked her again and again if she was sure, but Star had been determined. Within weeks, Amin and she had become allies and she now considered him one of her most loyal and trusted friends as he guided her through royal etiquette and protocol. And, surprising to almost everyone, she hadn't caused an international incident. *Yet*.

As another wave of tiredness hit, she yawned, despite the excitement thrumming through her veins. They were supposed to be heading into the desert with Nadya, Nayla and Khalif's parents and, although she would absolutely love to go with them, she wasn't sure she was quite up to it.

Star had been there when Khalif had revealed the suite to the twin girls, and been half deafened by their squeals of excitement and squeezed as hard as six-year-old girls could squeeze with their love and thanks. Surprising both their uncle and their grandparents, Nayla had been the first up the tree, while Nadya had had to be bribed away from the bathroom, but both loved their bedroom equally. Hafsa and Bakir's eyes had sparkled with tears of gratitude and love and Khalif had held her hand as if he would never let her go.

She heard the sound of bare feet stepping out onto the balcony and turned to see her husband, her Prince, her King, standing there with nothing but a towel wrapped low around his hips, making her instantly dizzy with desire.

He smirked as if he could read the shockingly intimate, passionate thoughts running through her mind as he walked towards her and pressed a kiss to her forehead.

'I know we're supposed to be going to the oasis, but you look exhausted.'

'Gee, thanks!' She laughed, playfully slapping him against his big broad shoulder, the secret flickering in her chest burning away the tiredness and brightening her with expectation and excitement.

'How are you feeling?' he asked, his hands burning a trail of desire down her back and over her hips. Her pulse picked up and her core throbbed with need, but she pushed that all aside for just a moment.

'Pregnant,' she said, smiling, knowing that Khalif was half distracted and it would take him a moment to—

'Wait, what?'

She looked up at him, a smile wide on her lips, loving the strong connection between them, their gazes locked, hers filled with confidence, his with wonder and disbelief.

'I'm pregnant.'

His hands went to her hips, his fingers gentle against the ever-so-slight bump, but his eyes had not left hers. His gaze searched hers in the same way he'd always done, as if awed and unbelieving that he'd found her, that she had chosen to be his and would always be his.

'I love you,' he whispered against her lips before pulling her to him and kissing her with all the love she could ever want and more. And in all the years to come, all the time they had together, she never felt anything but cherished, wanted and loved.

* * * * *

LET'S TALK
Romance

For exclusive extracts, competitions
and special offers, find us online:

*Calls cost 7p per minute plus your phone company's price per
minute access charge